Lost With Leo

Shelley Munro

Munro Press

Lost With Leo

Print ISBN: 978-1-99-106385-4
E-book ISBN: 978-0-9941433-8-9

Cover: Kim Killion, The Killion Group, Inc.

Munro Press, New Zealand.

First Munro Press electronic publication April 2017
First Munro Press print publication May 2025

DEDICATION

For Paul, my husband, partner in crime, and fellow adventurer.
Every day is a good day.

INTRODUCTION

Driven by revenge. Felled by a woman...

Leo Mitchell wants to contribute to the operating expenses of the new family-run Middlemarch resort, which specializes in capture fantasies for female guests. Betrys Torin offers what Leo thinks is a wonderful opportunity, but in reality is potentially deadly. He hungers for vengeance. A capture might be the perfect payback...

To protect her son, Betrys must procure men for her alien employer Iseult Orna. She hates her job and loathes the guilt she feels at trapping the sexy Leo into signing an irrevocable contract. Even worse, she has started dream walking and sharing passionate sex with the gorgeous man. She's smitten, yet knows they have no future, because when Iseult catches up with Leo, he'll die.

Inside scoop: Iseult's appetites for men are extreme. Because of that experience, shifter Leo starts out as a sourpuss, but Betrys knows he's just the cat's meow.

PRONUNCIATION GUIDE

Many of the alien characters within these pages bear Celtic names. Here is a guide to help pronounce their names:

Betrys Torin – (bee + trice) tor + in

Iseult Orna – (ee + solt) or + na

Alana Orna – (ah + lah + nah) or + na

CHAPTER ONE

SPIDERUS MANSION, DALCON CITY, PLANET DALCON

"Good night, sweetheart." Betrys Torin kissed the top of her son's head.

Ricci's young face glowed with an impish grin as he slid beneath the white covers of his sleep-bed. "Good night, Mama. Don't be sad. Everything will turn out all right."

Her breath caught, but she forced her lips to kick up at the corners. "I love you, Ricci." She ruffled his hair, gave him another quick kiss on the cheek and retreated to her quarters with mere seconds of her allocated deadline remaining.

She hated her situation, hated it with a passion, yet despite her constant planning, her scrimping and saving, her search for alternatives, freedom was no closer.

Trapped.

Betrys prowled the interior of her room, her heart beating faster than normal. How could everything turn out all right when she'd made such a colossal mistake and placed her son and herself in the way of inescapable danger?

With no answers, she paced herself to exhaustion. In the distance, a timepiece struck to mark the cycle segments. It grew late and she needed to rise early to prepare things for Leo Mitchell's visit to Iseult, her employer.

Leo.

The backs of her eyes stung as she shrugged off her robe and climbed onto her sleep-bed. At the last second, she reached for her oracle cards and did a quick three-card spread. The door to romance was the first card she drew and a hoarse laugh of disbelief shot up her throat.

"Goddess, please. You're playing a joke on me." *Romance.* Any man in her life belonged to Iseult. Even her son, until she managed to extricate herself from Iseult's web.

In disgust, she thrust away her oracle cards. "Lights off."

Her small room plunged into darkness, and she pulled the covers over her nakedness. She closed her eyes and forced herself to relax, to sink into the arms of sleep.

A bright swirl of colors drew her like a beacon. The hues pulsed and glowed, and she found herself enticed to follow.

Not awake.

She knew she was sleeping, but she'd never experienced anything like this before.

Scarlet red. Emerald green. Royal purple. Cobalt blue.

The vibrant colors should've clashed, should've hurt her head with their wild, crazy swirling, but instead, she found herself stumbling toward the pulsating ball. It stopped moving at the top of a hill by a lone tree. The ball split into separate colors, and each one pulsed. A crossroad, she realized.

Betrys studied the four different colors and chose the green one. The instant the decision firmed in her mind, the other balls blinked from sight. The green broke into swirls and strands, and they wound around her arms and legs, her torso, guiding her to the right.

Betrys found herself outside a bedroom, looking through a window at a huge sleep-bed. The covers were turned back as if waiting for the occupants to arrive. And there *were* two people because the sweet perfume of flowers, the soft music, and the bottle of nectar-wine nestled in a chill-sleeve hinted at a couple.

The door to romance.

Part of her mind wanted to snigger at the impossibility, yet a sense of wonder held her in thrall.

A dreamscape.

Spoken of in hushed tones by her people. At least before the war wiped out most of her race. Not every person experienced the dreamscape. The ability skipped generations, sometimes more than one. Some families never received the gift. Her grandmother had been a skilled dream walker, but the talent usually manifested during the first years of sexual maturity, Betrys thought in confusion.

She'd married, had a child, and not glimpsed a single dream during the years prior to her union. The power had passed her by, and the lack of hadn't mattered since her marriage made her happy.

Drawn forward, Betrys padded through the open door and scanned the seductive scene. Her heart thumped extra hard while her mind probed the possibilities, the signs of the future contained in the dreamscape.

A sound from behind had her starting, and she whirled, her hand pressed to her breast. She stared at the man standing before her, swallowed, and gave a soft, pained groan.

Dreamscapes give hope, child. Her grandmother's gentle voice poured into her mind, almost as if she were in the room, almost as if she hadn't died cycles earlier.

Betrys sucked in a harsh breath, steeling herself against the shot of the guilt, the searing pain as she acknowledged the truth. She was pretty sure this dreamscape was a big, fat falsehood.

A nightmare.

"What are you doing here?" Leo Mitchell folded his arms across his naked chest. His lower half was garbed in tight black trews that displayed his flat midriff and the bulge of his manhood, but his feet were bare. Strong feet. Big feet. "I said, what are you doing here?"

Betrys frowned and lifted her chin. "I don't know."

"Fuck, I can't even escape you in my dreams."

She felt the furrow between her brows deepen as she cocked her head. "What do you dream of?"

"I dream of home," he said. "I dream of running across the paddocks with my brothers and friends. I dream of my girlfriends. I dream of hot, kinky sex."

Her breath caught, and somehow, the robe she'd worn during the journey here vanished, and she stood in front of him, naked.

She watched his gaze flicker up and down her body, linger at her breasts. Her best feature, according to her husband.

Leo prowled closer. He reached out with his right hand and smoothed his palm over her shoulder. His mouth twisted, and his attention shifted from her to glance at his groin. The growing erection indicated his interest, and he laughed. The sound held irony, a touch of disbelief.

"I haven't had a hard-on since you signed me up to service Iseult."

Betrys opened her mouth to refute his claims, then decided to remain silent. Nothing she said would change the truth. Both of them were ensnared in Iseult's web and neither would emerge whole.

Fact.

"I'll hate myself in the morning, but I might as well take

advantage of the situation." His gaze sought hers then, bright green like the orb that had led her here and full of mockery. "On your knees."

Betrys wanted to protest. She wanted to rail at his disrespect and the way he was ruining a perfectly good dream. This moment was important, and he was sullying it by his attempt to subjugate her, make her less.

But look what you've done to him, her conscience whispered.

That decided her, and without haste, she knelt before him. "Wish your trews away."

"What?"

"This is a dream. You control your thoughts." Not quite the truth, because she didn't understand how she'd ended up in a bedroom with the scene set to seduction. That made no sense at all.

His clothes dissolved as she watched, and his heavy erection spilled free. She glanced up to meet his green gaze. His expression held a dare, and something cracked inside her.

In that instant, she accepted her attraction to Leo, the hopelessness of it after what she'd done to him. But in this dream world, nothing could touch them because in the morning, they'd both wake in their sleep-beds on different planets.

She reached for him, noted the faint tremor of her hand, but kept going until her palm grazed his hip.

"Touch me."

His daring tone told her he thought she'd balk, but she slid her fingers over his warm skin until she reached his groin. His cock twitched at her first touch, and she thought she heard a muted groan. With her confidence growing, she handled him with more assurance. She took his hard flesh in her hand and stroked. This time, his moan of pleasure wasn't in doubt. His cock grew larger as she teased him and tightened her grip.

Betrys went up on her knees and guided his shaft to her mouth.

She used her tongue to trace the tip. His salty flavor exploded across her taste buds as she took him deeper, the act making her feel strong and intrepid. One of his hands settled on her head, a heavy yet welcome weight because it meant he was responding. Her private fears that she repulsed him were untrue—at least on the dreamscape.

Beneath his cock, his balls tightened, and she massaged them, fascinated because her husband and their race had smaller gonads with much of the testicles hiding inside the body. More practical, it was true, yet this difference brought a new element to her explorations. Her busy hands investigated while she took him deeper.

His big frame trembled, yet he remained rock-solid on his feet. He groaned with each suck, each teasing sweep of her tongue, and his fingers tangled in her hair, his hands subtly guiding her to take him faster and deeper.

In this dream, there was no gagging, no apologies because she couldn't do it right. On the dreamscape—at least this one—it seemed only pleasure existed.

The taste of him intensified, and his shaft grew even larger. Leo let out a growl and encouraged her to take as much of him as she could. She swallowed, and he grunted. She swallowed again and followed it up with a hum of recognition. This man, with his indomitable spirit, fascinated her. She admired his courage and she realized if she met him here again, she'd do anything he asked.

Leo's grip tightened on her head, his fingers yanked on locks of her hair. Another of those sexy moans issued from his throat, and he came in long, hard spurts.

At first, the shock of his semen hitting her throat made her still, then she swallowed on reflex, enjoying doing this personal act because it was Leo.

His grip loosened, and he pulled from her mouth. Without a word, he hauled her to her feet and led her over to the sleep-bed.

With a gentle hand, he pushed her down, and she fell, legs splayed in an unfeminine fashion. She tried to bring her knees together, to arrange her body in a semblance of dignity.

"Don't," he barked at her.

Astonished, she glanced at him and stilled. He sported a weird twist to his mouth as if he couldn't quite believe the situation or what had just happened.

Times two, she thought. And that was an understatement.

When she remained unmoving, his attention traveled to the spot between her legs. "Scoot over," he said, and relief swamped her fears.

Every dream held meaning, and this one was beyond weird. Or maybe not. Once she'd signed up Leo, part of her had hated handing the contract over to Iseult. She'd wanted Leo for herself. Obviously, on the dreamscape, she felt confident enough to claim him. She sighed at the vagaries of her world. Goddess, she might as well enjoy the experience since sex with Leo would never happen in reality.

Leo hated her, and his future was limited since Iseult would kill him at their next meeting. The Spiderus woman murdered all her lovers, and there was nothing either she or Leo could do to change his fate.

"You're not my normal type," Leo said, breaking the silence that had fallen.

"What is your type?" she asked, startled by the fact he was speaking to her. Normally their interactions were confined to stony silence and accusing glares.

"I enjoy confident women. Women who are comfortable in their own bodies and dress accordingly."

"You dislike my robes?"

"They help you blend into the background."

The camouflage was a defense mechanism, a requirement around Iseult. If she behaved like furniture, she became part of the décor, and she raised her chances of living to see the next day and her son.

He stared at her a fraction longer before dipping his head and claiming her lips in a kiss. She expected ferocity. She expected anger. She expected punishment.

Leo Mitchell surprised her with gentleness and seduction. He traced his tongue over her lips, learning the shape of her mouth. His quick nip of her bottom lip surprised her. She gasped while he took advantage of further exploration.

He gathered her closer, pressing his muscular chest against her breasts. The sensations tumbled over her. Softness against hardness. Female against male.

His breath carried a faint tinge of mint while his scent held an addictive herby aroma that brought to mind open spaces and freedom. She wrapped her arms around his broad shoulders, wanting to wallow in the sensations of touch and taste and scent.

The sole person to touch her these days was her son, and Iseult monitored their meetings. The woman wanted to keep her slave and procurer locked into her contract, under her control.

It worked, and Betrys fell into line without argument. Anything to keep her son safe.

Leo slapped her shoulder, the sting giving her a fright rather than pain. "Don't wander," he ordered. "I'm here. I don't know why or how, but I'm here, and for some reason, I want you. We are going to have sex, and you will stay with me every step of the way."

His glare was dark green and fierce, yet strangely, she wanted to laugh. Confusion filled him as much as her—two lost souls stumbling on the dreamscape.

"Don't let your mind roam, or I'll stand and walk away." The tight set of his face told her this was no idle threat.

"I'm sorry," she said and meant every word. She should—they should—enjoy this opportunity because the chances were they'd both die at Iseult's hands.

12

Unpalatable but true.

Decision made, Betrys relaxed. The instant their lips met, hunger exploded, and she rolled, taking him by surprise. Grinning, she continued to kiss him, but now her hands wandered too, charting masculine territory. Sleek, sexy muscles. Hidden strength. His chest, stomach and back bore scars from his two sessions with Iseult, yet they'd healed to blend more naturally with his skin tone.

She trailed kisses down his throat and took a teasing nibble from the fleshy part between shoulder and neck. He shuddered, making a gasping sound as she dragged her tongue over the spot she'd nibbled. His erection went from interested to rampant against her leg.

Fascinating.

An erogenous zone.

She nibbled again, but this time, he groaned and rolled her beneath him. He ravaged her mouth now, seemingly intent on drawing a response. Goddess, driving her to madness. Already her quim moistened for him, her pulse slammed in happy anticipation, and she couldn't stop trailing her fingers over his warm skin. The man was pretty, yet not in a feminine way. He'd snared her attention from the first and continued to fascinate her with his bravery and cool belligerence.

He intrigued Iseult too.

"Right, that does it," he snapped. He moved so fast that a surprised squeak emerged from her, and seconds later, she found herself dangling over his knee, staring at the floor. His hand slapped her bottom, the sting sending ripples of shock scooting across her skin. Before she could process, could react, he smacked her butt again with two quick swats. She gasped a rapid breath, unsure and off-balance. Myriad bursts of discomfort ruptured her feel-good mood.

Pain.

More shock, this time with a thrilling edge of dark heat.

An impudent finger made a quick foray between her legs, and his grunt suggested her wet folds pleased him.

"Are you going to focus on me?" he demanded.

"Yes," she said quickly. Too quickly.

"I'm not sure I believe you." He punctuated his words with another smack.

"Ouch!" *By the goddess.* She attempted to squirm free and he let her. She stood to put a healthy distance between them before sending him a haughty look. What sort of dreamscape let a man punish a grown woman in such an embarrassing manner?

"Come here."

"Are you going to strike me again?"

"No." He paused, and she swore the air shimmered between them.

Intrigued, she inched closer. Without warning, he grinned, and the tension leached from her tight muscles. Her bottom smarted now, but she wouldn't feel a thing once she woke.

Leo wrapped his arms around her and lowered his head to kiss her. Once again, the kiss was soft and tender and sent messages diving to her quim. His hands wandered her back, her bottom. Nimble fingers stroked and delved until she moaned with enjoyment, craved his possession.

With ease, Leo lifted her and set her on the sleep-bed. His mouth fastened around a nipple. Part of her had wondered if he'd be a lazy lover because he wouldn't need to put forth much effort to get a woman. But maybe the dreamscape worked in a different manner. She had no one to ask about the intricacies of dreams or their interpretation.

He drew hard, and the sensations flared, pushing her into easy compliance. At least until he started to lift his head. She gripped his skull and tugged on his long black hair. It was soft and fragrant and she loved the way it spread around them in a dark curtain.

"More," she gasped.

"I'm going to give you more," he promised.

Without haste, she released her grip and snared his gaze with hers. His green eyes sparkled, the pupils flattened slits rather than round. Weird, but he was from a different planet.

She set about exploring him, searching for differences. He had nipples—two of them, although she understood the women of his race fed their young. She'd have to ask questions—no, maybe not. The other difference she discovered was the color of his testicles. Her husband's had been less visible, and they'd gone blue on arousal.

Leo's balls had hardened and risen beneath his cock. She'd been too enthralled with tasting him earlier to notice the more subtle changes, but she did now.

"Finished exploring?"

"Yes, thank you."

"Good." He rolled her, taking control of her arms by holding them above her head while he feasted on her mouth and her breasts again. By the time she lifted her head, sobs of pleasure and demand spilled past her lips.

"Now," she said. "Take me now."

Leo remained silent and used a muscular thigh to spread her legs farther apart. His nostrils flared, and a wash of embarrassment flooded her because the scent of her arousal perfumed the air.

Then she forgot her discomfort. Leo guided his cock to her entrance and thrust with one forceful stroke. She gasped at the drag of his shaft along her sensitive tissues and angled up her hips to receive his second drive home. More. She craved more of this unbearable friction.

Goddess, she'd missed this so much, missed her husband. She tried to hold on to the thought of her husband and his gentleness, but Leo shoved the memories aside with his vigorous plunges and his demanding personality. Her hands crept from above her head to clutch his back.

"Leo," she cried out, the enjoyable sensations sapping any inclination to fight his dominance. Each touch was so good. The swell of pleasure grew and expanded until she thought she'd explode, unable to contain all the emotions within her physical shape. Leo withdrew, thrust and hit her clit at the perfect angle to make her implode with ecstasy. The blissful feelings tingled and sparkled inside her for long, long moments, and once they started to ebb, the tension released from her muscles.

"You look beautiful when you come."

Her eyes snapped open, and heat collected in her cheeks. The knowledge that he'd watched her throughout brought a rush of vulnerability. "I...don't look at me."

"Why?" He stroked into her, lazy and unhurried, then withdrew to repeat the move.

A shudder took her, another low-level climax already starting to build. A shocked gasp escaped her, and his eyes narrowed.

"Something wrong?"

"I'm going to come again."

His grin was a flash of sharp white teeth. His thrusts continued but at a faster pace.

She hadn't seen him smile before. No, that wasn't true. She'd seen him smile once in the market—her first glimpse of him. She stared and thought she saw something spark in his eyes before he closed them and shut her out.

His thrusts were rapid now, and she gripped his shoulders, raised her hips, and strained for her second climax. It burst over her, sharp and quick but still breath-stealing. Leo came with a shout, the wash of his seed warm in her quim.

Amazing, she thought. Her senses worked better on the dreamscape. Everything was brighter and sharper, the scents evocative while the feelings lingered because her backside still throbbed from Leo's hand.

Leo pressed a kiss to the sensitive spot where shoulder and

neck met, this time giving her a hint of teeth. The man seemed fascinated with that particular part of her, and she had to admit his raspy licks and nibbles pushed a raft of agreeable sensations to the fore. He could do that as long as he wanted.

He kissed her without haste. The kiss was sexy. It was passionate and pulled an appreciative groan from deep in her chest. She closed her eyes to concentrate on the sensations and felt as if she were flying.

Leo lifted his mouth, and she smiled. Her body jerked, and she was conscious of dropping, falling. A thump. Her eyes flew open, and she found herself on the white tiled floor of her small bedroom in Spiderus Mansion.

A dream.

A visit to the dreamscape.

She pushed to her feet, aware of a smarting on her buttocks. She rubbed them and gave a rueful grimace. While she'd dreamed of Leo spanking her, the bruises would come from her tumble to the floor.

In the distance, a timepiece chimed, and she realized it was almost morn.

"Lights on. Half power," she mumbled in defense against the blinding illumination. The purity of the white fried her gaze, and she squinted while she donned her robe.

As she hurried to prepare Iseult's morning meal, she wondered what the dream meant. Had she truly visited the dreamscape, or had her guilty conscience come into play because Leo Mitchell's inevitable death weighed on her mind?

The Dalcon spaceport was crazy busy. Leo Mitchell scanned the crowds of locals and alien tourists who thronged the arrival hall and toyed with the idea of hitting someone. Perhaps one of the big red dudes with swirling tentacles around their heads. Their meaty fists looked as if they could do some damage. If he were injured or unconscious, he'd have a good excuse to miss his appointment.

Leo pondered his scheme and dragged his hand through his hair, pausing as his fingers met a hat. Oh yeah. He'd shaved off his long locks. Scowling, he straightened his cap.

Hell. This picking a fight was looking better and better. *How hard would they hit?* A black eye, a wired jaw, a plethora of bruises decorating his body. He imagined the repercussions, and his shoulders slumped. He had to keep his word because he needed the final payment to get the farming side of their enterprise fully operational.

No alternative.

Leo hefted a backpack over one shoulder and navigated a path through the mass of travelers. He circled the Red Mumber males despite the urge to lash out and punch them in their muscled midriffs. Innocents. They didn't deserve his problems heaped on their heads, not after he'd walked into the trap under his own steam.

Beware of petite women bearing gifts.

His mouth twisted as he dodged two upright aliens with pale-blue skin. That was one gift horse he should've punched in the mouth. Worse, he'd fucked her in his dreams last night, spanked her pert arse because she hadn't focused on him.

Weird.

He wanted to hate her—hell, most of the time he did detest her—but in his dreams he fucked her and enjoyed the experience. All kinds of messed up. A shrink would have a fun party with that screwed-up scenario.

He sidestepped a kid—at least he thought it was a child—as the hard-shelled creature scuttled past on all fours. One last meeting. All he had to do was endure this last session with Iseult Orna, collect her money, and head back to the resort, a man free of obligations.

One final session.

Leo sucked in a deep breath and exited the arrival hall.

Makeshift stalls bordered the streets and created jams in the pedestrian areas. Fly-scoots darted overhead, avoiding the hordes of people, but facing problems of their own as they jockeyed for airspace on their journey through the city. Market day was profitable for some, but it made for volatile crowds and short tempers.

Up ahead, the crowd jostled a stooped and wizened woman. Several Tigrus youths, recognizable by their striped skin, hooted with laughter as the woman's shopping flew through the air. Bright-pink fruits spilled from a bag and rolled along the rutted cobblestones. A jar of liquid struck the ground and shattered in an explosion of white.

Leo glared in the youths' direction and stooped to pick up as many of the woman's possessions he could find. "Here you go, ma'am. How far are you going?"

The woman was even older than he'd thought. Her face was a mass of lines, and she had one large milky eye instead of two like him. It blinked as she regarded him. Alarm jerked in him, a wince in reaction, and he broke their gaze. That was plain creepy.

"To the corner," she wheezed. "My shop is there."

"Let me carry your shopping for you," Leo said.

"Thank ye." Her bony hand fastened around his arm, and he fought to maintain a pleasant expression. She not only looked and sounded old, but she smelled ancient—a combination of dirt and moldy leaves with a hint of green to freshen her scent and push it a tad above disgusting.

She leaned on him and moved at the pace of a snail in ponderous steps. The journey to her shop stretched along with his disquiet. He unlocked the door and helped her inside. The building appeared dingy from the outside but bore a clean and ordered interior. Much bigger and cavernous than he'd expected. Herbs and dried flowers hung from hooks and perfumed the space. Transparent boxes and jars held things foreign and creepy. His attention snagged on one. Were those dried fingers?

"Thank ye," she said again. "Can I offer you refreshments?"

"No, I'm fine. I was glad to help you, but I have an appointment." Leo turned away, unease pushing him to haste.

"Wait." The woman's hand shot out, and she gripped Leo's arm, her fingernails digging into his flesh. "Let me give you some advice."

"Advice?" Leo's skin crawled, and he had to force himself not to bolt.

Her gaze bored into him, equally horrifying and magnetic. *Scary as hell*. "Today will be hard, boy, but you will live where others have died."

Leo's stomach bucked, the remnants of his coffee and chocolate roll eaten at the resort sloshing in an alarming manner and threatening to charge up his throat. How could she know what he intended to do today? What was expected of him? "I don't know what you mean."

Bright red swirled into her eye, combined with the white, and bled into pale pink. "Listen to me, boy. You will survive. Don't let revenge blacken your heart and make you so blind you can't accept what is in front of you." Her fingers tightened on his arm. "Remember what I say, boy. Don't let revenge take you over. Now let me give you some tonic. No charge," she added before he could argue.

Leo nodded even as his mind tried to reject her words.

She hobbled over to a shelf, appeared to ponder her choice, then reached for a glass vial. After pausing again, she reached for a second. "This will help you recover. Drink entire vial. One now. One after." She pulled out a stopper and handed the glass vessel to him. "Drink," she urged.

Leo scrutinized the vial then figured *what the hell*. God, the liquid smelled revolting. He glanced at the woman, and she gave a small nod of encouragement.

She wasn't going to let him escape without drinking the stuff. He took a quick breath and gulped the contents. His stomach pitched and roiled, and he swallowed urgently to keep down the tonic.

"Good. Good." She cackled, displaying a gap in her bottom set of teeth in her amusement. "Put other in jacket pocket. Drink after."

Sharp teeth, he noted, and shuddered as he stuffed the vial in his pocket. Some of these alien types were freaky. "Thank you. I'd better go or I'll be late for my appointment."

"Thank ye, boy, for a kindness to an old lady."

"You're welcome," Leo said with the manners ingrained by his parents, and with a last polite smile, he stalked from the shop. His rapid breaths evened out as he stepped into the street to merge with the market crowd. The semi-fresh air helped to settle the rocking and rolling in the pit of his stomach. Instead, a strange warmth filled him. Peculiar, but not unpleasant. He continued to his destination.

Iseult Orna lived in the better part of the city, near the palace. Her mansion stood at the end of a cul-de-sac with no near neighbors. A tall stone fence kept unwanted visitors out, the razor wire running along the top and security guards punctuating her preference for privacy.

The closer he came to the palace, the harder he needed to work to force his limbs to function.

Fear.

It was a tight band around his chest, restricting his breathing until it felt as if each breath emerged and entered through a straw.

The mansion came into sight, and each inhalation sawed into his lungs. He forced his tense limbs to carry him to the gates, to ring the bell for entrance. A voice squawked from a concealed speaker, and Leo backed away in quick, jerky steps, the flight response kicking in big time.

Run. Run. *Run!*

Yet his promise to honor a contract kept his feet firm, and he stated his business in a steady voice. "Leo Mitchell to see Iseult Orna."

The gates bearing the crest of a spider parted and slid back with nary a sound to allow him entrance to Spiderus Mansion. Leo strode up the driveway, past the gardens, to where a petite woman waited for him. A brown mouse with brown hair, brown eyes and a secretive nature. She looked as if she wasn't capable of spitting at a fly, let alone hurting one.

He knew better.

A snarl rumbled up his throat, and if he could've shot flames with his eyes, she'd be burning in hell.

Betrys Torin.

She was the traitorous bitch who'd lured him into this trap with her timid yet persuasive ways. His hands clenched at his sides. Weird, but she was also the sexy siren whom he'd fucked in his dreams. Confusion about the way his brain fired lately was an understatement. He loathed Betrys for getting him into this situation with Iseult Orna, yet during his dreams last night, he and Betrys had rolled around together naked, did decadent things to each other...

He shook himself, squared his shoulders and took a deep breath as if preparing for battle. In a sense, this was war.

Sure, Iseult Orna was beautiful, but her heart was as black as her hair and her sexual predilections were far from normal.

He'd been cocky during their first meeting, a little arrogant, but Iseult had soon slapped the swagger out of him. Shocked, traumatized after their first fucking, he'd tried to backtrack and renege on the deal.

Iseult, backed up by her muscle men, had disabused him of the notion, so he'd turned up for the second fucking and healthy payment. A fine tremor went through Leo, even though he struggled to maintain an impassive façade. The second encounter with Iseult had been even worse.

This third and final session might just kill him.

CHAPTER TWO

A *whoosh* of relief swelled in Betrys Torin's chest, along with a serving of embarrassment. Her dream last night...

She shook herself and forced her mind to the important topic of the day. Leo was here. After the second meeting with Iseult, she'd had to help him don his clothes and stagger from the mansion. Part of her had wondered if he'd refuse to attend to Iseult's needs for the third and final contracted session. It had happened before, and she, along with several of Iseult's guards, had enforced the contract. No matter which way the third time went, the man would die.

She registered Leo's wariness, the clench of his fists and the jerky steps, as if he had to force himself to enter the grounds of Spiderus Mansion. She felt her heart twist.

"Good, you're here and on schedule." Betrys shrugged away her sympathy, her sorrow at losing her dreamscape lover, and hardened her resolve.

It didn't matter what she wanted.

At least dying in Iseult's bed was the lesser of two terrible alternatives. Iseult's guards would tear him limb from limb and gnaw on his bones. Goddess Juna, even thinking about it made her stomach bubble with nausea.

"You warned me what would happen if I reneged on my contract," he said, his voice toneless, while his dull green gaze accused. "I need the currency."

But he wouldn't receive any shillars for his last session. The currency would go to his family because he was dying, although he appeared stronger than the others. He'd walked into the mansion grounds under his own steam. Iseult would be pleased.

He removed his hat, and she gaped at him for long seconds.

"What did you do with your hair?"

"It kept getting knots in it. It was annoying in the heat of Ione so I shaved it off."

Iseult would hate the small mutiny. She favored her men strong, powerful and sexy. The prettier the better. Like Leo. "Iseult is preparing for you."

His features went to hard rock. "Do you enjoy your job?"

Betrys ignored his question, tried to discount the sense of him standing so close. She thought about the beautiful man way more than she should. And the dreamscape opening between them...

"We shouldn't keep Iseult waiting. It makes her angry." She turned to walk away.

He grasped her shoulder, and a shudder sped from her head to toes. Thankfully, his hand dropped away almost immediately. Why this one, she couldn't guess, but the pride in him, the way he straightened his shoulders even though he knew what awaited made her admire and desire him.

Leo—she'd started thinking of him as Leo after last night on the dreamscape—moved closer and sniffed her neck.

Betrys jerked away before she caved and touched him. "What are you doing?" Did he just sniff her? Iseult had a distinctive scent. Most men found it attractive, but the idea of smelling like *that* woman brought revulsion. It was bad enough she was forced to work for her, but to become similar to Iseult, even in a small way, raised her gorge. She swallowed. Once. Twice. Hastened her footsteps so he could no longer see her expression and worked at gathering her scattered control.

This man rattled her and had done so from her first glimpse of him in the Dalcon marketplace when he flirted with an old Tigrus woman. Now her powers had kicked in, and she'd visited him on the dreamscape. Useless to fight destiny. *But Goddess Juna, destiny had made a mistake. She'd failed to understand the message contained in the dream and today her dream lover would die.*

Her throat tightened, and she struggled for emotional balance. Handsome. So handsome he made women stop and stare. Goddess, she'd gawked at him, and she'd detected other females smitten by the sexy man. He hadn't noticed that he'd created a pedestrian traffic jam around the fruit seller's stall. With his height, his long black hair, his powerful physique, and the perfect symmetry of his features, the package was attractive, but add the stunning pair of jade-green eyes, and he'd made folk of both sexes gape.

Yes, the man was handsome, and because of his stunning good looks, she'd approached him with an offer he couldn't refuse. Once he knew the bargain came with strings, it had been too late since Iseult's web had him trapped.

"You're not the same species as her or her guards. Why do you work for her?"

Because she had no choice.

Betrys ignored him and led the way into the mansion via the servants' entry. It was quicker and would get Leo to the central web before Iseult arrived. She liked to make an entrance, dressed to impress, and if she wasn't admired in the correct manner, life became difficult for them all.

Hard fingers curled around her upper arm and hauled her to a halt. He spun her around to face him and repeated his question. "Why do you work for her?"

None of the sexy and demanding dream lover showed in his face, but her grandmother had told her the male often fought destiny and pretended their dreams didn't exist and therefore couldn't be real.

"She pays well." A lie, but the faint curl of those perfect lips told her he'd believed she'd signed him up for money. "Hurry. We need to prepare you before Iseult arrives."

"And everything Iseult wants Iseult gets."

"Yes," Betrys said in a thick voice, and she couldn't meet his gaze.

Betrys hurried along the servants' passage and turned into Iseult's private quarters. In the sanitizer room, she turned to Leo and started to unbutton his shirt.

He slapped her busy hands away. "I've been dressing and undressing myself since I was five years old."

Betrys let her hands drop away. Her son preferred to dress himself too.

In the distance, a timepiece chimed midday.

"Please hurry, or Iseult will punish all of us." Goddess, she couldn't keep doing this, couldn't keep luring men to their deaths. It was killing her inside, and with Leo, the situation magnified. Her desire for him dueled with her love for her son. Today they would all lose. Battling tears and despair, she swallowed hard. "Please, Leo."

His face didn't soften at her plea, but he did start removing his clothes. He disrobed without a fuss, which she appreciated. He'd lost weight, something she hadn't noticed during her visit on the dreamscape. The suction marks Iseult inflicted on her lovers had healed and almost disappeared. Unusual. The oddity would intrigue Iseult.

Without being prompted, he walked into the sanitizer and started to cleanse in preparation for his meeting with Iseult.

Goddess Juna. *He was going to die today.* Guilt and despondency soaked her pores, filled her thoughts, weighed her down. He had people who loved him, and they'd never learn of his fate.

"Are your family on Tiraq?" she blurted, even though she knew the basic details.

He glowered through spiky dark lashes. "Why do you want to know?"

Betrys gulped. Telling him she wanted the information in order to inform his loved ones of his demise didn't seem tactful or wise. "Just passing conversation."

His contemptuous snort echoed and brought the heat of distress to her face. She averted her gaze while he completed the cleansing and drying process and picked up the silky white robe Iseult insisted her lovers wear.

"I have four brothers and one sister," Leo said. "Is that for me?"

"Yes." She opened it for him to slide his arms into the sleeves, but he snatched it from her and donned the garment by himself.

Betrys gasped, yet couldn't fault him. If she wore his shoes, she'd feel the same distrust, the same contempt and hatred. Understandable.

Their dreamscape ties counted for nothing. They couldn't. She needed to protect her son. Iseult would order her men to kill Ricci if Betrys refused to carry out her orders. In her own way, she was trapped like Leo, except hers was a living hell. At least Leo would have the peace and tranquility of death.

Iseult Orna bubbled with anticipation. This latest food offering purchased by her maidservant tasted exquisite. His essence still fizzed through her system, which was unusual in itself.

She stalked a circuit of her private rooms in an effort to burn off her excess energy. It was a pity the last feeding always killed them because this one—this one was something special.

Too bad. She'd savor this session, extract every bit of his essence and enjoy the high that came with the fucking. Such a beautiful creature. Perfect of face and form.

Faint vibrations thrummed beneath her feet and danced in the air, alerting her to the fact Betrys was delivering the man to the main web. Excitement pulsed in rhythm with her rapid central valve, and fangs sprang to prominence in her mouth.

She hadn't looked forward to a feeding so much for eons.

Her in-home com buzzed.

"Yes?" Iseult barked.

"The man is ready for you," her maidservant said.

"Perfect. I am very pleased with your latest procurement. You may take tomorrow off and visit with your son."

A faint gasp rippled from the com, and Iseult's lips curled into a benevolent smile. She was a reasonable being after all.

"Thank you, mistress."

"Make sure you are back by fall of dark to carry out your duties."

"Yes, mistress."

Her maidservant's smooth voice never faltered or changed in register, but if Iseult troubled herself to pull up the screen for her private cameras, she was certain she'd spot the woman's distaste. A melodic laugh spilled free at the thought. Her maidservant disliked many of her duties, but she performed them anyway because Iseult had custody of the woman's young son.

A cute wee thing, and much prettier than his mother.

Iseult had told Betrys she would release her son, and they could be together again. Her maidservant believed her words when her intentions were quite different. The child would make a tasty snack with more years of seasoning. Oh yes. While it was true the Spiderus race could not lie and always spoke the truth, they were canny enough to leave out pertinent facts. Those not of the Spiderus race did not comprehend the subtleties of the game.

Iseult let out another delighted chuckle and sauntered to the looking glass to check her appearance. She picked up a jeweled comb to place in her dark locks before replacing it on her dresser. No, the decorative comb would be too much and would clash with the colors of a well-fed Spiderus pulsing across her torso. An unusual occurrence but very exciting since it meant she was capable of breeding.

"Despite what my clan thinks," she murmured. "A child."

Smiling with satisfaction, she pursed her lips and blew a kiss at her reflection. She plucked her favorite flogger off the corner of her sleep-bed and strolled from the room.

Time for dinner.

CHAPTER THREE

L eo stood in the center of the round room, in the exact position Betrys had instructed him to wait, and every muscle in his body urged him to flee. Thing was he suspected his legs would fail to hold him upright long enough for an escape. Apart from last night, when he'd dreamed of fucking the mousy Betrys, the white-covered walls, the floors of this room, they featured in his nightmares—colorless except for his vivid red blood.

"Why hello, pretty," a sultry voice said from the doorway.

Leo sucked in a harsh breath.

Too late. Too late. Too late to run now.

Footsteps—small, sharp clicks against the tiled floor—stiffened his spine. Then came the slap of a flogger against the flesh of her hand—her warm-up tool. Leo swallowed, the sound audible, and her seductive chuckle confirmed she'd heard, noted his fear and gloried in his distress.

The flogger sounded again.

Slap. Slap. Slap, against her palm.

Then silence fell, apart from the click of her heels as she circled him, her gaze a slow slide of friction across every inch of his skin. To his horror and disgust, his cock started filling.

"You have healed well," she crooned. "Much better than the others."

Still, Leo kept his eyes closed, not wanting to see the beautiful face, the one that covered the depraved woman beneath the slick surface.

The flogger whistled through the air, the *slap, slap, slap* against her palm harder now, as if in displeasure. Leo was certain he knew what had disturbed the woman. His bald head.

Too late, bitch.

Leo gathered a bundle of memories in his mind—good recollections, the very best. Him shifting for the first time. Playing with his brothers in the town of Middlemarch on Earth. Making love to his girlfriend. Cathy had died during the initial virus outbreak. He ditched that part from his memory capsule and tossed in every other happy occasion he could recall, every recollection of days and nights when he'd experienced happiness.

"Why did you cut your hair?" she asked.

"It-it was in the way." Fuck, she'd reduced him to stutters.

"I liked it."

She'd enjoyed yanking on the long strands and using them as a bridle, but he never uttered the thought aloud. Less was more with this evil bitch.

"Tell me the truth," she demanded.

"It was h-heavy and hot."

"Hmm, I sense truth in your words. Though not stupid, I. You wanted to annoy Iseult. Truth?"

"Truth," Leo spat.

Before he could open his eyes and follow up with a glare, the flogger swished again and struck his arse. Pain sparked along his nerve endings, sucked the ire out of him, and left him quivering. Defeated.

"Pity," she cooed, but it was in a dispassionate voice. "But it will matter little in the end. I will still have my way with you."

The flogger whistled in a series of quick blows. Each rained on a different part of his backside. Each throbbed and pushed pained groans up his throat. Each lash arced like electricity to his cock, to his balls, and filled him with shame.

Difficult to understand how he hated the woman, yet her actions had his body behaving like a begging dog.

"Open your eyes. I want to see your pain, feed from your fear."

Leo forced open his eyelids, met her avid gaze. Up close, her eyes were a weird blue and he saw himself reflected, counting six likenesses. She could see behind her, but her distance vision was poor. Not that the knowledge helped him to escape her clutches.

"Good." Her breath was hot against his neck as she leaned forward.

Leo tensed, knowing what was coming next, but he wasn't quick enough. Her fangs sank into the base of his neck and sucked on his flesh. He shuddered, fighting the euphoric sensations propelled into him from her bite.

A moan whispered from his lips, and he relaxed against her curvy form, letting her take as much of his lifeblood as she deemed necessary. She wouldn't kill him this way, at least he didn't think so. No, she enjoyed toying with her prey.

Teasing and taunting until he screamed.

And he would scream.

He wouldn't be able to help himself.

Her smile was gloating and bloody when she lifted her head. Her gaze had darkened from deep blue to black, a sign of her growing arousal. She stepped back and he staggered. Blood trickled from the bite at the side of his throat. It ran over his collarbone, down his pectoral muscle and dripped to the floor. Brilliant crimson against the white tiles.

"Stand in position," she barked.

Leo attempted to straighten. His knees gave before he caught his weight and spread his legs to hip-width as per her order. Slowly, he lifted his arms. His muscles trembled with the effort, and he wondered how long he'd last. Didn't matter. She flayed his skin with her flogger, taking bites from any spot that attracted her attention. He sucked in a slow breath. That bloody straw again. No matter how hard he tried, he couldn't seem to force enough oxygen into his lungs.

She circled him, those bloody heels of hers *tap-tapping* on the tiles. He heard that sound in his nightmares, woke screaming because he thought she was in his bedroom.

The *tap-tapping* ceased.

Slap. Slap. Slap.

He winced at each sharp blow of the flogger against her palm. Soon he'd feel that bite against his skin again and the deceptive power of it. If not for his feline genes, he wouldn't heal.

"Eyes open."

He nodded.

"Answer me." The flogger struck his right shoulder, leaving a fiery path of pain in its wake.

"Yes, Iseult." Her name left a dirty taste in his mouth.

"Better."

She walked into his field of vision, her gaze avid and disturbing. Fuck, she made him feel unclean, both inside and out. He couldn't wait to crawl into a sanitizer unit.

"Does your cock feel tight?"

"Yes, Iseult."

She kneeled at his feet and ran a fingertip along his shaft. His body jerked, both with fear and desire. Her pointed black tongue traced her bottom lip then she tipped back her head to smile at him. "I think we'll do something different today."

Fear slithered through Leo like a stealthy serpent. Sweat beaded on his forehead, collected in his armpits. He stared at her but panic colored his vision. Different was *not* good in conjunction with this woman. His breaths rasped in and out and a silent scream broke out inside his head, deafening him. The urge to close his eyes was almost too much for his restraint.

She rose and surveyed his tense muscles, his rigid posture. Her cheerful smile widened, and she let out a sharp, high-pitched cry.

Her Spiderus minions scampered into the circular room on all fours, their small, round heads alert yet submissive. Hell. He couldn't look at them, wouldn't look at the spider version of them without a shudder. He was beginning to understand his sister's dislike of the hairy insects. If he could ever talk to her about this experience, he'd tell her the larger version was even more hideous.

"Prepare the mating bed," she ordered.

The minions hesitated. Maybe in confusion because she wasn't following the usual path of torture and sex. The skin on his backside was hot and tight, but it wasn't bloody yet. She hadn't struck his cock with her flogger as she had during the previous sessions.

"Now," Iseult snapped in a hard voice. "Make haste, and I'll allow you each one taste of his blood." Her black tongue slid over her pink lips, and she made a smacking sound. "It's delicious."

The minions scattered like flies disturbed on a carcass. Leo's biceps trembled from holding his arms in the air.

"You can put your limbs down, pretty Leo."

Hearing her say his name was another shock. She'd never, ever used it before, had always objectified him. Fuck, did this mean he'd pleased her?

A whimper sounded in his mind, and she issued a delighted chuckle, making him realize the cry had been real. His knees trembled and gave way without warning. He crumpled and dropped to the ground.

Iseult laughed again, a shudder of what looked like ecstasy shaking her frame. She stalked away, leaving him curled up on the cool tiles.

Click. Click. Click, went her heels. Leo moaned. Even though he couldn't see, every scuttle, every tap, every slap amplified, echoed through his head and screamed of danger.

"Perfect," Iseult said. "Escort Leo to the mating bed."

Leo tensed at the increased scuttling, jolted at a sudden high-pitched shriek.

"One taste. No more," Iseult warned. "Any warrior who dares to take more will suffer instant death. Put him on the mating bed first."

A hairy black hand grasped his forearm, jerked him off the floor. Leo tried to retreat, but a second minion grabbed his other arm and propelled him toward a round white bed. Their rancid scent, lightened with a touch of a green herb, made his stomach swirl. Nausea ripped up his throat and exploded from his mouth. Once he started throwing up, he couldn't stop. The sounds, the scents crowded in on him. His heart beat so fast he thought the organ might pound right out of his chest. The minions holding him released him, and he fell onto the firm bed.

A series of shrieks filled the air, fast and choppy and indecipherable. Furious.

A hairy arm grasped him again, dumped him on the floor. His head struck the tiles, and everything went black.

"That is disgusting," Iseult said. "Primitive creature."

Her head of security grunted. "What to do?"

"Clean the mating bed. Clean him up and get him in position. No instance of wastage once he gains his senses."

"We can still taste him?"

"Same terms. One taste each."

Her security man gave a curt nod. "I understand. One taste."

"Call me once he's ready. I will be in the tranquil web."

"Yes, mistress." The security man nodded. "It will be done."

Iseult sauntered away. At the doorway, she snapped her fingers. "With me."

Betrys came to attention, and Iseult saw her fall into step behind, the perfect slave as usual. Her mind slid to the male. Such an exquisite taste to his life force. His semen too, although she'd yet to taste that today.

A frail creature.

A pity this final meeting would kill him.

Leo came awake with a hard jolt, his panicked cry echoing in the creepy white room. He tried to shift his arms, failed. God, the crazy bitch had paralyzed him.

A piercing squeak close to his ear had him starting. He turned his head to come face-to-face with one of the minions. Its hairy hand crawled across his chest in a loverlike caress.

Leo yelled, tried to squirm away, but his arms and legs were bound. The black hand moved to the spot where Iseult had bitten him. The hairy fingers prodded gently, and Leo relaxed a fraction. Then the creature lowered its head and lapped its black tongue over the wound.

He let out a panicked croak, tried to jerk away, but the minion had him in a tight embrace. The mouth suckled once, just once, before the Spiderus male lifted his head. He shifted aside, and Leo relaxed until another moved into position beside the bed. Fuck, they were each taking one sip of his blood.

Leo grabbed for his memory capsule. Playing at the beach. The hot sun shining on his hair and skin. The surf crashing to shore. Eating ice cream to cool down on a summer's day. The sexy dream he'd experienced with the mousy Betrys as his lover.

The suction at his neck annihilated the flimsy walls created by his memories. God, they were feeding. They were feeding on his neck like vampires. One hard suck, then they gave way for the next minion.

Finally, finally the line ended, and he was left alone in the white room. He swallowed, his pulse racing because he knew Iseult would return.

His mind drifted. He tried to revisit his memories, but all he could think of was Iseult. Instead of happy memories, fear stalked his mind. He trembled, beads of nervous sweat breaking out on his forehead.

Then he heard the *click, click, click* of Iseult's shoes coming closer and closer.

The footsteps grew louder, approached the bed.

"Open your eyes, pretty Leo." Her voice was soft, almost gentle, but Leo wasn't fooled. If he disobeyed, he'd suffer more pain than he could imagine.

Leo followed instructions, but instead of meeting her gaze, he stared at the white over her shoulder. Endless white. It was like sinking into infinity. God, give him color, even if it was his own blood.

She huffed, but laced the sound with humor. He amused her—at the moment.

"Silly, pretty boy. Admire spirit. Enjoy yours." She shook her head. "I always get my way."

She unbuttoned her white leather jacket to reveal a tiny white camisole thing below. His gaze returned to the whiteness while his insides quivered in apprehension. While the males had hairy black skin, Iseult's was smooth and creamy white. He heard her peel from the matching trousers with ease. Leo had never known anyone who did that. Leather was a prick of a fabric to wear and get out of later. She made the process appear elegant and sensual and somehow, she managed to keep on her shoes.

Leo continued to stare into the white, attempting to distract himself because now she intended to touch him intimately. She'd take his cock into her mouth and suck hard. It would feel good at first but soon her pointy black tongue would lick one time too many. He'd become ultra-sensitive and crazed with the pain. Enough to put a man off sex. It had put him off, and apart from taking the mousy Betrys in his dream, he hadn't had a normal woman since his first meeting with Iseult. Three long months, and once he left this room, he wouldn't want another woman for a long stretch.

He caught a flash of color, of emerald green and cobalt blue. Intrigued, his gaze tracked the brilliance.

Distraction.

Holy fuck.

The color came from Iseult. Her body. Instead of creamy skin, her torso was vibrant. Bemused, he stared until her sultry chuckle jerked him from his stupor, reminded him he was restrained and at the mercy of an alien spider woman.

Leo shifted his weight, tried to relieve the tenseness of his limbs, the ache of his backside pressing against the unforgiving surface of the bed. God, his dick was so hard. Pre-cum beaded his slit. Had to be something she'd injected into him with her bite. Didn't get this much of a hard-on any other time...

"I pretty, Leo?" Her arched brows indicated a question.

"Yes," he croaked, even though *peculiar* and *fuck-ass weird* fitted the situation better.

"You please me, pretty. A pity..." She gave a delicate shrug of her toned shoulders and crawled onto the bottom of the bed. Her smooth fingers ran across his foot, her touch swirling his anxiety higher. His breath caught as her perfume—musky like sandalwood—filled his air space.

She lowered her mouth and traced her pointed tongue over his big toe, bit with sharp teeth. Licked away the blood.

No. No. *No!*

Leo felt his pulse rate jump and fought his urge to shroud his sight. Her fingers followed along one calf, she bit there too. With each nip, it were as if an army of fire ants marched over his flesh. His heart pumped faster and faster. Tears formed and rolled down his cheeks. At least she'd put that damn flogger away somewhere, hadn't brought it to her mating bed.

She took a bite out of his inner thigh and glanced up to study his cock. His breath caught. Another tear trickled onto his neck. She saw it, smiled and reached for it with her finger, *tsking* at his flinch.

Her smile widened to reveal her pointed teeth, the stark whiteness of them against her black tongue. She licked the droplet off her fingertip and studied him, a wrinkle of thought on her pale brow.

"What is the magical ingredient? I've never felt so well." She seemed to lose interest in his tears and lowered her head to delicately trace one nipple with her tongue. 'Round and 'round, then a brief foray across the hard disc. She rubbed along his leg, leaving a trail of slimy arousal. Every part of his leg where it spread started to ache in concert with the areas she'd bitten, yet still his cock saluted with interest.

She bit into his pectoral muscle without warning, and he grunted, jerked against his ties.

Then she turned, presenting her back. Dread stalked him then because she was unpredictable. She straddled his waist, and all he could see was the brilliant patchwork her upper torso had become. Emerald. Cobalt. Hints of scarlet.

Her back bowed and he felt her hot mouth surround the head of his dick. The initial pleasure gave way to the fiery swarm. He grunted, fought the urge to seek refuge in his mind. She'd see. She'd be watching him in her peripheral vision.

Suddenly, Iseult shrieked. The high-pitched cry lifted the hairs at the back of his neck, made him aware of the clamminess of his skin. She froze then shrieked again without warning, the sound vibrating along his cock. The bright colors peeled away like a zipper to reveal a hairy black body.

Her third shriek held a victorious tone. She started to suck on his cock, no longer toying with him. Extra arms and legs unfolded and gripped him. Leo stared, too horrified to look away now. Two arms cradled a smooth white ball. Iseult hissed around his cock, licked and sucked, and the fiery pain seemed to subside.

Leo felt the beginnings of a climax and didn't try to hold back. The sooner he came the sooner this nightmare would end. The suction increased and a black finger pressed on his perineum. Another finger slid up to his rear entrance, pressed and pushed inside. Leo thrashed beneath Iseult, his dick withering a fraction in her mouth. She never hesitated, and somehow, the intrusion didn't hurt as much as he feared. To his great relief, some kind of lubricant eased the way. He hated to think...groped for his stash of happy memories. Started during his fifth birthday party. The bouncy castle. The pony rides. The smiling, creepy—

Fuck.

Iseult touched a spot that sent electricity jolting across each and every nerve ending. He cried out, pain and panic making him thrash, and she shrieked in triumph. Her probing finger stroked back and forth over the sensitive area. His balls tightened and fiery pleasure forged a path up his cock. Iseult gave another shriek, her teeth sinking into the head of his cock even as her finger continued to stroke and stroke and stroke.

His heart thumped hard. A roaring sensation crashed through his head. His muscles twitched at the stimulation while his mind screamed. Too much. *Too much*. The pleasure rose and swelled until he wondered if the shell of his body could contain the rush of sexual hunger.

The instant he thought he might hurtle into climax, Iseult bit his dick and knocked the wave lower, only to massage his sweet spot and send him soaring again.

SHELLEY MUNRO

Leo heard screaming, and took long, long moments to realize it was him. The finger inside him stroked seductively, the sharp bite of teeth failed to halt the escalating pleasure. He shattered, saw stars hovering in the fringes of the darkness that spread over him like a tsunami. He kept coming and coming, the contractions taking long moments to tail away.

"Eyes open, pretty," Iseult crooned.

Sluggish, heart still trying to claw up his throat, he obeyed, focused on the far wall, and lost himself in the white.

She licked his limp cock, and to his shame and alarm, his dick started to fill again.

"Good boy," she whispered, and the horror began all over again.

Somewhere during the third session, he retreated to the birthday party and refused to leave. His cock hurt, every muscle—*every muscle*—throbbed in a rhythmic ache. He thought he climaxed again, then two of her black hands pinched his midriff. The pain sent the black swirling inside his mind. Horrid pain. Indescribable pain. So much pain. Something snapped and he tumbled headfirst into the black hole.

Falling, falling, *falling*.

He wondered when he might stop, hit the bottom, but he kept going, vaguely felt the pain increase, if that were possible. Was this death? Wasn't so bad.

Leo reached for the darkness, embraced its loving arms and went limp.

CHAPTER FOUR

Betrys couldn't escape the screams. Earsplitting shrieks. Hair-raising shrieks. Horrifying shrieks. Clapping her hands over her ears did nothing to mute Leo's anguished cries. Silent tears streamed down her face. Goddess Juna, what was Iseult doing to him? How long did she intend to prolong the man's agony?

Finally, finally the whimpers ceased. A chill prickled her skin, and Betrys wrapped her arms around her chest in an effort to get warm. She rocked back and forward, back and forward, back and forward, waiting for the summons that would soon come.

Leo was dead.

She'd lured yet another man to his death—not just any man, but one she'd met and interacted with on the dreamscape—and the weight of the knowledge made her want to curl into a ball and hide. While she didn't do the actual killing, she was complicit in Leo's death. It was she who trolled the marketplace and selected suitable specimens, she who enticed and offered the men great riches, she who acted the pimp.

Goddess, she didn't want to do this again, loathed the idea of repeating the process. But she would because of her son.

She'd do anything to keep Ricci safe.

The light of her life, and her one sole reminder of the man she'd loved and lost during the Colossium wars. Already, her young son showed signs of his father—the beautiful clear-blue eyes that told of power, the knowledge of the generations in his young face and a strength of character most people garnered with age. He would lead once he was older, if she could keep him alive.

She *would* keep Ricci safe and somehow extricate them both from this mess.

At least Iseult would keep her word. She wouldn't taste Ricci until he reached the legal age on Dalcon. She had a while to earn the currency to pay off her debt to the woman. A few cycles to recruit for Iseult—to bring her compatible males from which to feed.

The clank of a bell summoned her, and she jerked upright. She staggered, forced her will on her knees, and headed for the mating room. The deed was done, and now her task was cleanup and disposal...

She used the sleeve of her robe to wipe her face and sucked in fortifying drafts of air. Later she would mourn her dream lover, but now she had duties to perform.

Betrys hurried along the long passage. She came to a stunned halt in the doorway.

The minions were mounting someone, something. Lining up to mount her, and Iseult...

Betrys blinked and focused again. No, she wasn't mistaken. That was Iseult and she'd shed her skin, transformed into a creature resembling her minions. Much larger, but her normal face remained, pale and seductive, while her torso and legs were all black, hairy spider with bands of bright colors to differentiate her from the males.

Swallowing her horror, Betrys hovered in the doorway, unsure of what to do. Leo lay on the mating bed, his form still and bloody.

Dead.

A pang of deep anguish swelled inside her, pressed against her chest and tightened her throat until she thought she might suffocate with the force of the weight. Leo had fought with his available tools—attitude and belligerence. Once he'd signed the contract, there was one way forward since Iseult loathed cheating or attempts to renege on contracts. The second man Betrys had signed up had attempted to leave Dalcon without fulfilling the contract, and Iseult had sent her three best men to track him. They'd caught him, Iseult had given him a chance to return, and on his refusal, her men had killed him without hesitation.

Iseult let out a screech, and the last of her soldiers went flying. He picked himself up and scuttled with a lopsided gait in Betrys's direction. She stood aside and watched in bemusement as the rest of Iseult's men exited the room with the same unsteady gait.

Iseult meandered over to Betrys, her beautiful face wreathed in a bright, happy smile. Such a contrast to her repulsive body. *Eyes forward*. Betrys forced her horror to the back of her mind and pasted on what she hoped was an impassive expression.

"I am pleased with the pretty boy." She smiled at the still form on the bed, and not a shred of guilt or regret showed on her features, despite the cavalier way she'd tortured and killed an innocent man. "Never have I received enough man essence to go into frenzy. You have done well. Two thousand shillars bonus. We will celebrate tonight after I recover. Clean up this mess, and start looking for my next meal. If you find a similar male—one who pleases me as much, I will grant you a bonus. Ten thousand shillars."

Betrys felt her mouth drop open, saw the trace of amusement on her boss's face, and pressed her lips together. "It will be done."

"Consult Amos about the celebration feast. He will know what to do."

Betrys watched Iseult stumble away. The female Spiderus appeared drunk, and her smile... Betrys shivered. That contented smile shunted fear through her, but she attempted to keep her revulsion from leaking free since Iseult had peripheral vision.

A low series of squeaks came from the direction in which Iseult had disappeared. Was that singing? Creepy.

Betrys forced herself to edge farther into the web, one foot after the other. Iseult always referred to the web as the mating room, and she'd wondered why since death occurred in this chilling chamber of white. Now she understood. Iseult needed more...more man essence, then it became a mating room.

She stopped by a concealed cupboard and pushed a button. A door slid open to reveal a trolley, which she wheeled over to the bed. She scrubbed a hand over her face, steeling herself, pushing past her grief and regrets. Despite the crushing weight on her chest and her gut full of knots, she forced herself to touch Leo's naked form. He lay facedown on the bed, his corpse still and bloody and warm, and she jerked her fingers away with a harsh sob.

Self-loathing swept her, gathering momentum like an unstoppable meteor storm, until she trembled from head to foot. Another death to add to her total. Another death to weigh on her conscience and disturb her nights. *Another death.*

This one—Leo—was a hundredfold worse than usual.

The futility of escape ate at her as she stared at the spot of blood on her hand. She wiped the smear on her robe, and straightened her shoulders, lifted her quaking chin, anger rushing into her in a torrent. This wasn't right. She knew it, and Iseult must know it too. Goddess, how many years would she spend as the woman's slave? What if she never got away? Ricci could die in the same manner as Leo, then the entrapment, the deaths and the sale of her soul would be for nothing.

Aware Iseult would call for her soon, she lined up the trolley with the bed and steeled herself as she grasped Leo's shoulder to roll him. He was muscular and solid and she grunted with exertion. A shocked croak scratched up and out of her throat at her first real sight of his ravaged body. His injuries were worse than normal. His cock was red and bloody and still erect while his torso bore numerous bites. The worst wound was to his stomach, to the right of his bellybutton, where Iseult had left a gaping hole. Between the flesh and blood, she glimpsed a hint of white. Bone? Organs? Or something else?

Horror rolled back and forth from her mind to her stomach, gathering momentum until the soup she'd managed to eat earlier burst up her throat and onto the floor. Her chest rose and fell in rapid sobs before she struggled to regain control. She averted her gaze from the wound, hauling and shoving at his inert corpse until he lay on the trolley. Exhausted, she massaged the small of her back and flinched on seeing his face. Tears welled, hot and angry, and she brushed them away. Unable to look at him again without another bout of bawling, she hurried over to the storage cupboard to retrieve a sheet to shroud him from sight.

Her white robe bore a dozen splotches of blood, and the vivid scarlet of it, the coppery scent of Leo's life force had her clapping her hand over her mouth.

Not again.

She swallowed. Once, twice, trying to tamp it down. Goddess Juna. She clenched her jaw and heaped silent curses on Iseult, but couldn't stop the rush of nausea. She turned away and vomited on the floor until her stomach muscles protested. Her breath came in hoarse pants, and her mouth tasted as if a Dalcon black bum-bug had crawled in there to die. She swiped the back of her hand over her mouth and straightened. A weak groan spilled past her lips.

Something else to clean up before Iseult summoned her. At the thought, she hurried to the intercom and buzzed Iseult's personal chef.

"Iseult requires a celebration feast."

"When?" Amos, the chef, asked.

Betrys rolled her eyes and prepared for a diatribe. "Later this evening, once Iseult has recovered from her mating."

"How the frack am I meant to cater for a feast without supplies or advance notice?"

"Iseult is the boss." She jerked her frame upright in a fighting stance. "I need to clean the web and deliver...something. Send a list of what you require to my genic-tab. I will return to the mansion as soon as possible and aid you with preparations."

"Don't make your promise an empty one." Amos slapped off the intercom, making it shrill in Betrys's ear.

"That went better than I expected." She glanced back at her trolley and her vision blurred.

Death, and her part of it, should have become commonplace—a means to acquire safety—but this broke her inside and the razor-edged shards dissected her psyche, ripping her apart. She'd admired Leo, the way he'd turned up as promised and approached Iseult with attitude. Not that his bravery had mattered in the end.

Leo Mitchell was still dead.

The man had family who'd wonder at his absence. She'd collected the details before Iseult took him for the first feeding. A sob escaped. It was easy to imagine their anguish and sorrow at his passing. She swiped away the rain of tears and wheeled the trolley along the passage to her private rooms. There she retrieved cleansing cloths and pulled back the sheet. Pride and decency wouldn't allow her to send Leo on his final journey to the goddess in this condition.

The scent of antiseptic cleanser sent her stomach heaving again, but she took small, quick breaths through her nose and began her self-imposed task. Iseult mightn't care about the men she killed, but Betrys felt compelled to give them the dignity they deserved.

With his back done she struggled to turn him again. She shoved and heaved, pushed and tugged, and managed to get him flat. Her quick gaze skirted his wounds, then she frowned. His erection had subsided. None of the other men...

She shook herself and reached for another cloth. Quickly, she cleansed his shoulders, his arms and legs. His cock... She hesitated, grabbed another cloth and briskly cleaned his groin area. *No different from bathing her son. No different from bathing her son. No different—*

Leo groaned.

Betrys started and let out a shocked *eep*. She backed up, hand and bloody cloth pressed to her breast. *What the goddess?*

Long, tense moments later, after staring at the trolley, the sound didn't repeat, and the tension eased from her muscles. No, bodies made noises after death. That was it. Nothing to alarm herself about. She inched closer, poked his thigh with one finger, and puffed out a breath when nothing happened. A light laugh emerged, filled with relief, a hairsbreadth from hysterical, and she resumed her task.

"You gonna rape me too?"

Betrys squeaked and scrambled backward, her feet tangling in the loose material of her robe. She struck the floor ass first and the pain on contact reverberated up her spine. Righting herself, she scuttled farther away until her rear hit the wall.

His eyes were open.

He was talking.

Leo is alive.

"You're alive," she repeated her thought, her mind navigating the tangled web of how and why. She came up with nothing that made sense.

"Feel like shit."

Betrys's thoughts skittered left and right, leaped over hurdles before she came to a conclusion. "Shush, Iseult mustn't know you're alive."

"Why?" he gritted out, but he did lower his voice. "She fuck her men to death?"

"Yes. Always. No one has ever lived before."

He tried to move, moaned, his face contorting in a mask of pain.

"Quiet," she whispered, her mind jolting back into gear. "You must be quiet, otherwise I won't be able to get you out of here." She grabbed another cloth and resumed cleaning him while trying to form a plan. "I can wheel you out of here as normal. None of them will think anything of it. Do you have a shuttle?"

"Yes, at the spaceport. Everyone dies? What does she do to them?"

"She fucks them until they die." Betrys made no effort to pretty her words. "Quiet, let me think. You're in no condition to fly. Do you have anyone who can collect you?"

"No one knows where I am."

The man seemed to recover a fraction, although he winced with each jerky shift of his limbs.

"Let me get your clothes." Dead men didn't require clothes, and her habit was to toss them, but he couldn't travel home naked. "I doubt anyone will come in here, but I'll cover you with the sheet. Please remain silent and don't move until I get back."

Betrys tugged the sheet over his scowling face and hastened from the room. Goddess, Leo was alive. She checked her timepiece. If she hurried, she could deliver him to the spaceport. She'd have to hire someone to pilot him home because she doubted he'd manage the task without aid. She'd need to use her own funds, take currency from her stash, yet suddenly, she didn't care.

Leo had lived, and she wasn't going to let Iseult near him again. He'd fulfilled his part of the bargain and deserved his freedom. She winged a prayer to the goddess that his wounds—especially the one on his stomach—wouldn't putrefy and kill him anyway.

She snatched his clothes from the web and raced back. Her shoes slapped the floor, and her robe rustled with her haste. One of Iseult's guards appeared. She slowed and approached him with caution. Normally, they hissed at her, made a series of guttural clicks that raised the hair at the nape of her neck. This time, the guard ignored her presence. He wobbled past on unsteady legs, his squeaks similar to Iseult's earlier discordant tune.

Betrys waited until he disappeared before darting back to the room where Leo was stashed. She found him off the trolley and slumped against the wall. With an annoyed mutter, she shut the door and hurried to his side.

"I told you not to move. Iseult's guards patrol the halls. I never know if I'll see them. You might have attracted their attention."

"Needed to stand."

"Here are your clothes."

"Give me jacket."

"Let me help you with your trews and shirt first."

"Jacket," he insisted, his voice belligerent. He reminded her of her son if he wasn't getting his own way.

"Here." She thrust it at him.

He wobbled, and she rushed to help him balance. He was taller, his weight a burden, and she struggled to hold him upright.

"Fingers won't work." Frustration and panic laced his tone.

"What are you looking for? Let me find it for you."

"Vial in pocket. Need to drink."

"Sit on the trolley. If you fall on the floor, I won't be able to pick you up."

He seemed to see the sense of this and let her guide him back. He half fell onto it and gasped for breath. Droplets of sweat beaded his creased brow.

Once she was certain he wouldn't topple, Betrys searched his jacket to find the vial he was so worried about. She discovered it in his inside pocket. A small glass vessel containing a milky liquid.

"Do you want me to open it for you?"

"Yeah."

The pungent scent from the contents made her eyes water. Her nose wrinkled, and she held it at arm's length. "Are you sure you want to drink this?"

"Can't feel any worse."

Guilt surfaced to thump her over the head. She'd recruited him, reduced him to this. She breathed through her mouth and approached him to hold the vial to his lips. She tipped it, and he drank the foul-smelling liquid. He made a gagging sound and fought to hold it down. By the time he'd swallowed the contents, his face was the color of her robe.

"Do you want to lie down?"

"Yes," he muttered.

Betrys glanced at her timepiece again. "Which bay is your shuttle parked?"

"C2," he said, his eyes rolling in an alarming fashion.

She'd dress him on his shuttle. The longer they spent here, the greater the risk of discovery.

"I'm going to help you. I'll put your clothes with you and help you dress later. Then I'm going to wheel you out and load you on Iseult's fly-mo. You need to be quiet from the moment I wheel you out of here. Okay?"

"Yesss."

His face had taken on a green tinge, and he looked as if he might vomit at any second.

She arranged him on the trolley with his clothes and boots and covered everything with the sheet. She grabbed currency from her stash, and with a quick prayer to the goddess, she opened the door and wheeled Leo outside.

Although the procedure seemed to take ages, in reality, she made good speed. She spied several of the guards from a distance, and they all staggered and scuttled in the same drunken manner as the first guard and Iseult. Something strange for her to puzzle out later.

With Leo stowed onboard, she closed the door and piloted the fly-mo from the mansion grounds. Designed to seat eight, the vehicle was simple to operate, and Betrys used it often while undertaking chores for Iseult. Including the disposal of bodies. None of Iseult's staff would think it strange for her to leave the mansion. She'd stop by the market and grab the items on Amos's list along with some of Iseult's favorite treats to serve at the celebration later tonight. That might improve Amos's mood too.

Betrys programmed in the directions for the spaceport—not far from the market—and went to check on Leo. His chest was rising and falling in rapid and shallow breaths, but the green tinge had receded from his features. A spasm vibrated through his muscles, locking his face into a contorted mask.

Betrys gripped his arm to stop him falling off the trolley. If anything, he appeared worse. What the goddess had been in that vial?

The spasm tapered off, and she left him to operate the fly-mo during the approach to the spaceport. Her com squawked, a terse employee from spaceport control demanding to know her destination.

"Mitchell craft. Bay C2 delivery," she said and thanked her foresight for requiring each male to complete a form with details of their background.

"Go ahead," spaceport control said.

Betrys flew to the correct bay and parked by a medium-size shuttle. She put the craft in park and hurried to Leo's side. The spasms had tailed off, and now he sprawled like a weak newborn.

"Let me help you dress. Can you stand?"

"Think so," Leo muttered.

He lurched off the trolley and almost face-planted the floor. "Think you overstated." She gritted her teeth and struggled with his weight. Finally, she managed to prop him against the wall and yanked his trews from the trolley. His underwear would have to travel in his jacket pocket. "Lift your right leg."

He frowned then lifted his left.

"Okay. I can work with that." She eased the trews onto his legs and pulled them up. She wrestled him into his shirt and closed the fastenings. For a brief moment, she decided not to bother with his jacket, but he began to shiver. "Jacket next."

By the time she managed to cram his feet into his boots, sweat beaded on her chest and forehead and wisps of hair escaped her donut-bun.

"Okay." She shoved his underwear into his jacket pocket and slung her arm around his waist. "Let's get you into your shuttle, then I'll hire a droid to pilot you home. Someone on your end will need to return him."

"'Kay."

Betrys urged him to the exit. Everything was weird today, and she had no idea how long Iseult would be resting. She couldn't risk staying away from the mansion for too much longer.

Leo stumbled, despite her help, and fell. He hit the floor with a thud, his shoulders heaving in rapid pants.

Panic roared through Betrys as she bent to assist him to his feet. "You're too big. Too heavy for me."

"Can't...can't..." Leo's eyes rolled and the lights went out.

Goddess, he couldn't be dead now, not after all this...

Betrys rested her fingers at the pulse point in his neck and found a heartbeat. A shaky laugh emerged, and she pressed the heels of her hands to her cheeks. On wobbly legs, she rose. The droid would have to help her load Leo into the shuttle.

She hurried over to the hire desk and made her request. Thank the goddess. There was a free droid. Betrys tried not to think about the loss of currency as she handed over a large amount of shillars.

"What do you desire of me?" the silver droid asked on activation.

"I need you to come with me, lift some luggage then pilot a shuttle to Ione Island on Tiraq. I will write you a note. Deliver this to the owners of the Middlemarch Resort and they will organize your return to Dalcon. Do you understand?"

"Your orders are clear," the droid said in a high-pitched voice.

Betrys shivered. The droid's squeaks reminded her of Iseult's exultant singing. She gathered her wits. "This way."

Leo was still unconscious on her return. Concern had her sinking to her knees to check his pulse. His lashes fluttered at her touch, his lids lifting extra slow as if they were heavy and cumbersome.

"Not dead yet," he muttered.

"You're not going to die," she said in a fierce tone. "Help me take him to the shuttle."

"I will carry him," the droid replied. "Lead and I shall follow."

Betrys hurried to the shuttle door and pressed a button to open the door. It refused to budge. She tried again. Nothing.

"The door won't open. Do you have a key?"

Leo's head lolled against the droid's silver shoulder.

"Leo," she said sharply. "Leo. The door?"

He mumbled something intelligible.

"Handprint pad," the droid said. "Press his hand against the pad." The droid shifted position and Betrys seized Leo's hand. To her relief the door opened with a quiet whisper.

She stood aside and let the droid enter. "Wait while I write the note, then you can leave for Tiraq."

"As you order." The droid set Leo in the seat and secured the harness.

At least he is an advanced model, capable of basic thinking, Betrys thought as she trotted off to procure a disposable genic mini-tab with which to send a message.

She arrived back at the shuttle, puffing and out of breath. "Give this mini-tab to Leo's family. I believe you will find them at Middlemarch Resort."

"It will be done," the droid said, accepting the mini-tab.

"Thank you for choosing Zionible Transport for your travel requirements."

Betrys took one last look at Leo. He was slumped in a passenger seat, only the harness holding him upright. Or at least that was the way it appeared to her. His eyes were closed again, and his chin rested on his chest. Intermittent spasms danced along his muscles, making him cry out.

Betrys bolted from the shuttle, but guilt followed like a tail. The door whispered shut after her and she hurried back to the fly-mo, regret chasing swiftly on her heels. But with remorse came a hint of satisfaction. If Iseult had realized Leo still lived she would have requested him for a fourth session and been within her rights. It was the way the contract was worded. And Leo would never survive another session with Iseult. Never.

Betrys imagined the intrigue Iseult would have felt. Yes, she'd done the right thing. She prayed Iseult never discovered her disloyalty.

Chapter Five

"Sir. Sir. We have arrived." A high-pitched voice spoke, inches from his ear.

Leo tried to lean away from the irritating squeak, but it droned on and on and on until Leo growled in self-defense. He cursed at the blast of light that seared his pupils.

"Sir?"

"Who the devil are you?" Leo asked.

"I am droid 765432, hired to deliver you and your shuttle to the Middlemarch Resort. We have arrived, sir."

Leo struggled to rise.

"Sir, should I remove your harness?"

"What?" Leo sent the droid a look, felt puzzlement, the loss of time in his own mind.

"The harness, sir?"

Leo followed the droid's gaze. "Oh." He gave a cautious nod in deference to the ball of pain perched in his head. The careful action tormented him anyway.

"I shall help you stand, sir."

With each squeaky syllable, Leo's head did a samba. "Fuck," he moaned when the harness released and his muscles needed to work to keep him upright.

A silver metallic arm wrapped around his waist and hoisted him to his feet. Leo's legs failed and his knees folded. If not for the droid, he'd have dropped to the ground.

"Have you been drinking, sir?"

"No," Leo gasped.

"Leo, you're back." Scarlett, his youngest sibling and only sister, skidded to a halt in the doorway of the shuttle. Her mouth dropped open, and Leo would have laughed if every part of him wasn't aching as if a cantankerous cow had kicked him good.

"Are you related to him? I have a genic mini-tab for you." The droid held him with one hand while he reached for the mini-tab with the other.

Leo dangled, unable to get his muscles to work without red-hot pain stabbing every muscle in his body. He jerked, trying to remain upright under his own steam, and moaned.

"You're bleeding." Scarlett tossed her black braid over her shoulder and leaned closer to survey him. She straightened abruptly, her sea-green eyes widening in alarm. "I'll get Saber and Felix."

"No." But his sister had already sped away. Now his older brothers were going to ask questions he couldn't answer.

"You are bleeding, sir," the droid said. "I will help you outside."

Leo felt the wetness at his stomach and glanced down to see blood seeping through his white shirt. He frowned, his brain sluggish as he tried to remember how he'd received the wound.

The droid helped him outside. Actually, no. The droid carried him outside because his messages to his legs refused to transmit.

His two brothers burst from the resort gardens with Scarlett following. Damn, it was bright out here. So bright, and he couldn't focus. His stomach was roiling, and the scent of blood filled his nostrils.

The droid halted on their approach. "Are you this man's family?"

"Yes," Scarlett said.

"I have a message for you." He handed the genic mini-tab to her and allowed Saber and Felix to take Leo's weight.

Leo groaned, despite trying to hold the telltale sound at bay. His head throbbed, he ached everywhere...even his teeth.

"What happened?" Saber's expression held concern. The oldest of his brothers, and the head of the family, he'd softened after mating with Eva. He wore his black hair shorter now, and his mate saw that it was neatly trimmed. The biggest change though—his mouth generally curved upward in a smile rather than dipped in a stressed frown.

"Did someone jump you?" Felix, his second brother, ran a hand through his military-short black hair, his grass-green eyes radiating equal worry. He must look as bad as he felt.

"Need to sleep." Leo got out the words with difficulty.

"Ma will want to doctor you first," Scarlett said.

"No," Leo barked. "Want to lie down."

"It says here that someone paid for the droid to deliver Leo here, and that we need to return him to Dalcon." Scarlett glanced at the droid for confirmation.

"Today or there will be additional charges," the droid added.

"The twins were intending to go tomorrow to pick up supplies," Saber said. "Go find them, Scarlett. Tell them to go today."

"Should I get Ma?" Scarlett asked.

"No," Leo said, his voice scarcely audible above the white noise in his brain.

He felt his brothers moving him, but kept drifting in and out.

So tired. Needed to sleep. Yeah, he'd feel better once he'd slept for a few hours.

"Where are we taking him?" Felix asked. "To Ma or to his quarters?"

"His quarters," Saber said. Leo was right. They didn't want Ma to see him like this. "Damn, he's out."

He and Felix carried Leo, following the back trail to the family quarters rather than going through the middle of the complex where guests might see and ask questions.

"He's losing a lot of blood," Felix said.

"Yeah. Shifting might help, but he won't be able to if he's going in and out of consciousness." What the fuck had happened to him? Saber knew there'd been something wrong, but Leo had brushed his questions aside.

Each week, he seemed to lose weight, and he'd shaved off all his hair a few days ago before taking off for Dalcon earlier this morning. His brother had become secretive, his temper uncertain.

In Leo's quarters, they stripped off his clothes and surveyed his wounds. There were scrapes and bites over a large portion of his body, a big wound on his belly and hip, and his dick looked an unnatural bright red.

"Fuck," Felix whispered. "What the hell happened to him?"

"I've never seen wounds like this before." Saber checked Leo's pockets, hoping to discover some sort of clue as to where his brother had been, and came up with a thick wad of cash. He held it up, and Felix whistled.

"That's a lot of money. Cage fighting?"

"The authorities shut them down. I haven't heard anything about an underground club opening. Besides that doesn't explain that." He pointed at Leo's groin and winced.

"I'll get Casey. She might have seen something similar," Felix said.

Saber nodded, concern for his brother a tight weight on his chest. He'd tried to get Leo to talk, and now he wished he'd persisted with his efforts. Maybe Casey would be able to help. Casey Seonaid, Felix's mate, had once been in the Dalcon military and had traveled the galaxy while undertaking her duties.

Felix hurried away, and Saber inspected Leo's wounds more closely. Although his brother appeared to be out, irregular spasms shook his frame. Saber's nostrils flared, and he caught a medicinal scent. Frowning, he straightened. Someone had cleaned Leo up and attempted to doctor his wounds. Someone had cared enough to try to get him home. But who?

"Hell." He hated to think of Leo's appearance before the mystery party had treated his injuries.

Felix returned with Casey, and Saber stood aside to let his brother's mate examine Leo.

"Scurvy sky pirates," Casey whispered, her brown eyes widening beneath the fringe of her brown hair. Her narrow face held intelligence and a fierce frown. "If I didn't know better, I'd say they were Spiderus bites. I've seen it once on the planet Voracious. The female of the Spiderus race kills her lovers. It usually takes more than one session, but she gets nourishment from their essence."

"Essence?" Felix asked.

"She drinks their semen and their blood. One of my men got entangled with a female. We found him dead, and the Spiderus woman had vanished."

"A Spiderus? So like a spider?" Saber asked. "How does that work? I sure as fuck wouldn't roll naked with a spider woman."

"From what I understand, they take on a humanoid form and are very attractive. It's only if they have a buildup of essence that they are able to revert to their other form and mate. At least that's what I've heard. There are a lot of rumors floating around, and it's difficult to discern between truth and fabrication."

"Christ in a campervan," Felix said. "What do we do?"

Casey moved closer and examined the largest wound. Leo moaned but never woke. "I don't like the look of this one. Is that bone I can see?"

"We need to wake him. Get him to shift to feline," Saber decided.

Casey picked up one of Leo's arms and took his pulse. "It's fast. Too fast. In this condition, I doubt he'll be able to shift."

"We could treat his wounds and let him sleep for a bit," Felix suggested. "Monitor him. He shouldn't attempt a shift when he's this weak anyway. The last thing we want is for him to get stuck in between."

Casey gawked at him and Felix. "You can get stuck? Why didn't someone tell me this?"

Felix went to his mate and pulled her against his chest. He tipped up her face and skimmed his fingers over Casey's cheek, his expression one of reassurance. "It's rare and only happens to very old or sick shifters. Occasionally inexperienced shifters too. None of us are in danger of getting stuck."

"Apart from Leo," she said. "You should tell Anna."

Saber scowled, exchanged a glance with Felix. "I doubt Leo will want Ma to see him like this."

"That's too bad," Anna Mitchell, the matriarch of the Mitchell family, said from the doorway. A tall woman with dark hair like her children, she vibrated with determination and mother-bear protectiveness. "Scarlett told me."

Saber stepped in front of her, held his mother in place when she attempted to duck around him. "It doesn't look good, Ma. He's too weak to shift."

Her gray eyes narrowed as she met his resolve with a glare. Her chin lifted a fraction. "I'm your mother. I've seen the best and the worst of all of you."

Saber sighed in defeat and guided his mother to the sleep-bed. She sucked in a harsh breath on seeing Leo's battered body clench in the midst of a spasm. He shuddered for long moments before slumping in a boneless heap.

"Did he say what happened?"

"He didn't say much." Saber's grim visage shouted his disapproval.

"Okay." Ma lifted her chin and gathered determination around her like a cloak. "We'll clean him up and let him rest. We'll need to take turns and watch him around the clock. The moment he gains consciousness, we'll encourage him to shift—if he seems strong enough to complete the transformation. Other than that, I don't see that there's much we can do apart from pray."

CHAPTER SIX

THREE MONTHS LATER, MIDDLEMARCH RESORT, PLANET TIRAQ

Another one of those bloody dreams. Exhausted from working with the twins in their new vineyard, he'd fallen asleep in his clothes. No sooner was he out than Betrys Torin popped into his head, enticing him, seducing him, fucking him during his sleep. On the brink of coming, he'd woken with a hard-on.

No more! Not tonight.

Leo stripped off his clothes and pictured his feline shape in his mind. The process took longer than it used to, and he had to use intense focus, the same concentration he'd required during his teenage years when new to shifting.

"Paint the cat in your mind, son."

The long-ago words from his father helped to soothe the angst that popped into his psyche more and more these days, the fear he might fail in his shift and end up between.

You can do this, Leo.

His father had been right, and it would be the same on this occasion. He imagined his cat, the sleek, muscular lines of his body, the prick of his ears, the swish of his tail, and finally, finally the magical prickles swept across his skin. Bones cracked, reshaped. Fur started to sprout along his back. The familiar pain racked his body, and he heard a grunt—his grunt—as the transformation took him. He dropped to all fours and embraced his feline form. His tail flicked back and forth, and his senses magnified.

The ever-present pain in his stomach faded as did the nagging ache at his temples. He left his quarters via the open terrace door and padded into the night air.

Tonight, the briny scent of the sea drew him. He wanted to play in the waves and sprint along the white sand. Feminine voices up ahead had him stepping off the gravel path and slinking into the undergrowth.

"Did you see the signs about the zylon creatures?" a woman asked. "Do you think they're as dangerous as they say?"

"They wouldn't have signs everywhere if it was a lie," another woman stated her opinion.

"I'm playing safe," the third woman said. "We're only here for a week cycle, and I want to enjoy every moment of the capture experience, not end up sick or dead because I didn't believe their signs."

Wise woman, Leo thought. Zylons were fluffy and cute, but their bites were deadly to most beings. Luckily he and his brothers had discovered the zylon bites had no effect if they were in feline form, and hunting them had become a popular diversion for the shifters.

The three women sauntered by him, dressed in slinky outfits

designed to impress. They were part of another batch of guests, drawn by word-of-mouth, to try the fantasy rooms and to indulge in the sensual treats available at the resort. The word *capture* filled the dining room, the reception room, the walkways. His top lip curled. Who knew he and his brothers would make a successful living by indulging women in their fantasies.

Sex on tap.

A dream come true for most males.

Not for him.

Leo dodged all of the women, stayed away from the resort and concentrated on the farming side of their operation. Their grapes were growing well, despite the tropical climate, and it would be interesting to see how the wine would turn out since typically the vines required cooler temperatures.

Once he was clear of the cluster of chatty guests, he trotted back onto the path to emerge on the beach. Colored lamps lit the sand, but the illumination didn't penetrate as far as the water. A night bird called from the trees, and Leo huffed out a sigh of contentment as he listened to the rush and tumble of the waves.

He ambled along the sand, heading away from the lit area, unconcerned about the inky darkness. His night vision was excellent. He, his brothers and their employees sometimes wandered the resort in feline form. Their guests thought they were pets, and after initial concern, seemed to become used to them.

A foreign sound jerked him to a halt. He cast out his senses, lifted his head to scent the air.

A woman.

Alone in the darkness, she was crying, her long brown hair a curtain hiding her face. He started to retreat, but something about the despondency of her sobs drew him closer. His nostrils flared, and he stilled again, eyeing her hunched form in confusion. Her scent—it was familiar.

He rifled his memory and stopped at a file he kept hidden, never dragged out and refused to speak of to his brothers. *No.* He inhaled again, a tremor sliding along his side. No, it couldn't be.

His feline wanted to run, wanted to hide, wanted to stay safe and secure.

The human part of him refused to flee. He had to know, had to discover if his senses were playing him false. His heart thumped, tripped, increased in speed as he slinked nearer.

A protest, a huff of breath emerged as truth gave him a swift kick at the glimpse of her profile.

He knew this woman.

Anger, pure and white, roared along his veins while he remained frozen in place. Wasn't it enough that she seduced him in his dreams? Oh no. Now she came to terrorize in person.

She hadn't heard him, was too wrapped up in her misery. He could be on her in seconds, his teeth biting, tearing, breaking her neck. She'd be dead before he got a good taste of her blood.

He stole one step closer, two steps, the urge to kill, to obliterate her from existence a siren song thundering in his brain. He trembled with the need to pounce, yet something held him back.

The repercussions for his family, plus he wanted—needed—to know why she'd lured him in with promises of easy money. Answers to make sense of her actions.

He sank onto the sand and pondered his options. He'd have to shift to speak with her, but instinct told him to hide his dual nature. He couldn't have explained why, yet he went with his gut. The longer he spent in feline form the better he felt. Besides, she wouldn't recognize him, which was an advantage.

Leo let out a growl of warning to expose his presence.

The woman's head jerked up, her brown eyes widened with a flash of fear. Then she relaxed on seeing the black cat and brushed her hair from her face. Her calmness spoke of close contact with one of his brothers or friends, and the knowledge had a snarl building in his chest. *No.* He forced away the unwelcome emotion and concentrated on his end goal.

Answers.

Payback.

Revenge.

While the scar on his stomach would never fade, at least he'd achieve peace of mind. Leo sucked in a careful breath and waited.

The back of her hand swiped over one eye as she knuckled away excess moisture.

Leo padded closer, senses watchful. Some of the women disliked the big cats, feared them, and if she ran after all, his feline nature would entice him to chase.

"Hey, kitty-cat," she murmured, her voice thick with sorrow. She held out her hand.

Leo considered biting, but again possible consequences for the resort had him obediently sniffing instead.

Every one of his muscles clenched when she dared to trail her fingers across his shoulder. His growl of protest stilled her hand.

"I'm not gonna hurt you, kitty-cat."

Too late. She'd already hurt him.

Betrys Torin.

Here at the resort.

The craving for action clawed him, urged him to proceed at breakneck speed. Women came to the resort for one thing. Sex and good fun. Some of them stayed, captured by his brothers and persuaded to remain as mates. Leo had never agreed with the idea—it cut too close to the bone. Betrys and her employer, Iseult Orna, had laid a trap, and he'd suffered for every minute of his naivety.

But now...now a plan formed in his mind.

He might have refused to take part in the resort activities, but for Betrys he'd make an exception.

Fury morphed to excitement at the concept of payback. Hell, apart from during his sleeping hours, he hadn't thought of sex, hadn't desired a single resort guest, but now blood pulsed hot and heady through his veins. The idea of this woman at his mercy.

He leaned into Betrys and drew her scent deep into his lungs. Hers wasn't a pungent fragrance like Iseult's but was spicy with the faint note of flowers and sunshine.

She petted him, her hand sliding along his spine, and he suppressed a shudder with difficulty. Her touch felt good—way better than it should—and the contrast with his ruffled feelings confused him. A purr erupted without his permission.

Leo redirected his thoughts. *Retribution.* It'd taste sweet, and maybe he'd nix his aversion to sex. At first he'd tried to act normal, as he had in the past. He'd danced with a woman and barely stopped himself from punching her when she'd groped his arse. After that episode, he'd stayed far away from resort dealings, and Saber let him, gave him the space he desired.

But back to the present. He'd follow her first, reconnoiter in feline form, then at the right moment, he'd capture her and show her just what it felt like to be helpless in someone else's power.

The dreams meant nothing. How could they? It was his mind fucking with him. A grunt emerged, a burst of unusual humor. He certainly fucked her during his sleeping hours, and now he'd do it in person.

Besides, he didn't trust her. She'd recruited him, drawn him into the spider's web, and he found it difficult to believe she hadn't done the same thing to other unsuspecting males. This would be payback for all of them.

Betrys sniffed hard and removed her hand from his back. Straightaway, Leo felt the lack of touch and grunted a soft protest. She gave a watery smile and fished in the pockets of her robe. Seconds later, she dabbed her eyes with a square of cloth.

Leo sank onto the sand beside her. A robe. Why the devil was she wearing a robe? The other guests wore as little as possible. In the fantasy rooms, they stripped to skin. At night, during the parties and gatherings, they wore tight garments, tiny dresses to display their assets. Why would Betrys wear a robe?

The hair along his spine lifted.

Had she come to the resort to recruit another sucker?

His brothers and cousins, his friends...

He cried out a silent protest at the idea. No, damn if he'd let anyone of his kind walk into Betrys's snare. He'd stay close to make sure she didn't sign up someone of his acquaintance.

Betrys stuffed her cloth back into her robe and resumed her stroking.

"I don't want to do this," she whispered. "It's wrong, but Iseult wants more men like Leo. I can't let her know Leo is alive and I've seen him." She sniffed, pulled out her cloth again while every one of Leo's muscles tensed.

What the devil did she mean? Three times. He'd fulfilled the terms of the contract. Fuck, there was no way in hell he'd let that monster bed him again. Weakness still struck him, and it galled when he couldn't keep up with his twin brothers. He refused to let his brothers or friends walk into the same trap.

"I don't want to do this, but I have to."

She remained quiet until Leo nudged her hand in silent demand and, after a shaky laugh, she resumed petting him.

"One solar week. How the goddess does Iseult expect me to manage this? Tell me that, kitty-cat. Iseult expects me to fall into line with her wishes..."

What wishes? Damn it to hell. Iseult could go fuck herself, because she wasn't getting her hairy hands or feet on him again. Not for a million shillars. Not while he had breath to object. *Not ever.*

Betrys sighed and climbed to her feet. Leo rose too and ambled after her. If a week was all he had, he needed to act fast. He'd follow her to her bungalow, then go see Saber. They could have everything set up for tomorrow night.

Hopefully he wouldn't have performance problems—he never did in his dreams—but even if he did, it wouldn't matter. He could still fuck her with dildos, make her desperate, give her a taste of vulnerability and a sense of the hopelessness he'd felt.

Saber would ask questions. He'd try to dodge the answers, but if he couldn't, he'd ad lib.

"You want to what?" Saber asked, his cool green gaze assessing and prodding.

"I intend to capture Betrys Torin in bungalow seven," Leo said.

"Why?"

"Because she interests me."

Saber leaned back in his chair, frowned. "You've been vocal in your dislike of our capture scheme. What's changed?"

"She attracted my attention. I intend to explore the possibilities, and I want privacy to do that."

"The capture camp is full for the next few days."

"Fuck." Leo's mind worked with computer precision, groping for alternatives. He had to do something now because a week wasn't long, and two solar days had already passed.

"I might have an alternative," Saber said after a short silence. "But first you need to tell me why this one. She's not beautiful, more dignified. I noticed her because of her robe," Saber added. "She sticks out like a weed in a flower garden. And she doesn't socialize or take part in any of the resort activities. Her behavior is odd." Saber maintained an even stare—waiting for his response—and Leo found himself wanting to squirm, to rush in to fill the empty pause. He controlled the impulse with difficulty.

"I met her on Dalcon," Leo said. "In the city."

"How?"

"I can't say."

Saber scowled. "Can't or won't?"

"Won't."

Saber scrutinized him then leaned forward to pick up his genic mini-tab. He tapped on several keys. "We don't have any detailed information about her on file. Just the basic stuff. None of the other men have expressed an interest in her because she is so odd."

Which worked to his advantage.

"Does she have something to do with your injuries?"

Careful, Leo warned himself. His brother was no dummy. "She hired the droid to pilot me back to Tiraq and got me to the spaceport."

"I see. So I'm mistaken about the whiff of lies in the air?" Saber's gaze drilled into him, but this was too important to muck up. Leo remained still and met Saber's gaze with unconcern.

After a long pause, Saber filled the silence. "You want to keep this woman as your mate?"

"I don't know yet." Leo surreptitiously rubbed his scar. For the last couple of days it had felt tight and tender to the touch. Only shifting and lounging around in feline form alleviated the ache. "I feel a stirring of interest. That's all. If I find we don't suit, I'll release her to return to her life on Dalcon."

Saber snorted, the abrupt sound tinged with humor. "A frisson of interest is where it started with me. With Felix too."

Leo kept his face impassive. He wouldn't be keeping Betrys Torin. On that count he was firm, but he *would* give her a taste of the same vulnerability and fear he'd suffered. He wouldn't hurt her, but she'd come to understand how it felt to be trapped and used. Spanking her in his dreams was one thing. Not much pleasure there, but in real life...

Yes. He'd tie her up and fuck her. He might spank her. While he'd return her hale and hearty, he could make her feel a little of what he experienced at Iseult's hands.

"All right," Saber agreed. "The deserted village I told you about. You can go there. It's habitable." He hesitated, traces of a smile lurking in his features. "There's more to the story than Eva and I told you. It's nothing bad. More startling."

"The disappearing shuttle?" Leo asked. Felix, Eva and Saber had told them about the shuttle they'd flown and how once they'd disembarked the vehicle had faded in front of them.

"That and more," Saber said. "You'll see. I'll help you capture Betrys and drop you off at the village. I'll give you three nights to decide if she's the one you want before I return for you both. How does that sound?"

Leo found himself smiling, a foreign sensation during the last few months. "That sounds perfect. Thanks, Saber."

Three nights to give Betrys Torin a taste of the mental agony he'd endured.

Let the games begin.

Betrys lay on the sleep-bed, willed herself to relax, but kept her eyes stubbornly open. Resist. Resist. *Resist.*

Though physically and mentally exhausted, she couldn't fight her mind's desire for sleep. The moment she toppled into slumber, the dreamscape summoned—a shiny enticement to cavort with Leo. With scarce thought, she found her body soaring along a swirly purple and blue path, a flickering jade-green light signaling her direction and final destination.

An instant later, she stood in front of Leo, her dreamscape the same luxurious room as before, full of color.

"Hi," she whispered as she approached him at the window. He didn't welcome her, yet he didn't shy from her touch either. She wrapped her arms around his waist, pressed her face against his back and drew in his scent. Masculine. Clean with a hint of herbs and spices. Just being with him calmed her angst, made thoughts of Iseult and the horrors of her days retreat.

During her past visits, he'd acted standoffish and fought their mental pull as much as she, but today he tugged her against his side and wrapped an arm around her naked shoulders. They stood in silence and stared out the window at the pristine white sandy beach and the rush of the jade-green waves. The sound of the water was soothing, and it sloughed away more of her anxious and fearful edges.

Leo drew her like a magnetic force.

Betrys didn't know if this was usual because, despite her research, she'd discovered no one with the ability to instruct her on the intricacies of the dreamscape. She'd never entered this world before she'd met Leo and had only instincts to guide her nightly journeys.

Without speaking, he turned her away from the stunning view and led her to the bed. Always the bed was covered with color, sometimes so intense the shades hurt her head. She'd tried to mute the vibrancy with splashes of white, but Leo always scowled at the white and overwrote her choice. She was sure this wasn't normal and wished her grandmother was still alive to ask. The dreamscape power came from her, she always went to Leo, and as such, *she* should control the settings.

With a gentle push, he guided her onto the sleep-bed and followed her down, trapping her with his muscular bulk. Helpless to resist, she wrapped her arms around him, drawing him close. Their mouths met, and everything righted in her world.

Sensations pelted her—the softness of his lips, the faintly abrasive stroke of his tongue, the rough calluses on his palms as his hands skimmed her curves. She melted—*melted*—under his ministrations, her quim blooming while her nipples hardened to tight points.

She ran a hand over his skull, which was a mass of short black waves now that his hair had grown. Her fingers trailed lower to the muscles of his back and settled on his butt. Their mouths dueled, teased, and clung in urgency. Her softness to his hardness. He lifted his head, and at his gentle nudge, she parted her legs.

"I'm gonna fuck you now. Slowly. Thoroughly, until you beg." He rose over her, his expression solemn as he guided his cock into place. With his gaze on hers, he slid home in a single stroke, and she felt the rawness of his emotions. His green eyes blazed with heat, and she relished his possession with every particle of her soul.

"Please. Please, Leo." Oh she wanted that, him, his total focus.

Happiness rose, swelling inside her while he thrust and withdrew, taking his time, despite her urging him to haste. She gasped at his next harder stroke, and gasped again when he reached between them to finger her clit.

"Please what?"

"I need you to...to touch me." She groaned his teasing strokes. "Yes, yes. Right there."

He glanced at her, and his breath caressed her face, knocked her equilibrium hard. A dream. She had to remember even though she was drowning in desire, a little confusion too because she didn't understand the purpose of these dreams. Part of her was still resisting while the other part of her thrilled to each of Leo's touches.

"Don't drift off. Stay with me." While his voice was harsh, his hands stroked with skill, keeping her on edge.

"I'm here." Even if she wasn't sure why.

Her nub pulsed, pleasure spiking sharply. Hungry little noises escaped her throat, and her orgasm exploded through her, taking her like a meteor storm. The spasms hadn't come close to tailing off when Leo climaxed too. For long seconds, he slumped against her, a heavy weight even in her dreams.

Betrys savored his sweaty body against hers. Any second now, she'd experience a falling sensation, and she'd wake on the floor. The fall explained her bruises, but it never enlightened her as to the lingering soreness between her legs.

Worst of all, she had no idea what the dream meant.

It never changed, never varied.

She arrived in the colorful room to discover Leo waiting for her. They made love, and soon after she climaxed, she'd find herself back in her room.

A burst of pain had her jerking away, and with a groan, she picked herself up off the bungalow floor. She glanced at her deck of oracle cards and sighed while she rubbed her aching hipbone.

Reading her cards shed no light on her dreams, and nothing changed. Nothing. She was still Iseult's instrument, the one that would send Leo to his death should Iseult ever learn he was still alive.

Betrys gave up eating her dinner of figus fish, shredded greens, and redmatoes. Even the signature dessert, the pavlova, tasted like dirt in her mouth, but she made a mental note to tell Ricci about the dish. He would have eaten her unfinished meal without difficulty.

"Excuse me," she said to the women at her table, and she headed outside for her usual walk. She stood aside for two Tigrus women dressed in their best sexy outfits.

"Did you see the blond man, long hair, big, big...shoulders?" The Tigrus's amusement came out *chuff, chuff, chuff.*

"No, no, no. I too busy ogling the two duplicates. I couldn't tell one from the other."

Betrys scowled down at her robe and wished it was pink rather than white so she'd blend better with the plants and trees. Her cheeks heated when she heard the Tigrus women's *chuff, chuff,*

chuff again, this time at her expense.

On reaching the beach, she stooped to remove her shoes and ambled along the damp sand in bare feet. If Corrin hadn't died during the war, her life would've been different. And her parents and younger sister who'd all succumbed when dissidents ransacked their house for food and valuables. If she hadn't lost them as well, she wouldn't have stumbled into Iseult's skillful trap.

If only. *If only.*

A lot of people had lost family during the war on Petros, and many of the refugees had ended up in Dalcon city, desperate for jobs, for food, and shelter. Some of them were reduced to begging in the market.

At least she had a roof over her head and plentiful food, even if she was essentially a prisoner. Even though Iseult kept threatening to harm Ricci, the truth was she had the luxury of time. Ricci wasn't old enough, and even Iseult never stooped to assault minors. But when Ricci came of age, things would change. Betrys knew this as well as she knew her last name. Iseult didn't pay her enough to buy her way out, not until this latest astonishing offer.

A cash bonus.

Her son versus Leo or one of his siblings or friends.

Goddess, she hated herself, yet she had to save her son, save herself. She couldn't worry about the man.

She sighed hard. Hindsight was such a bloody thing. Maybe she should have stuffed her pride in the depths of her robe pockets and offered her body in exchange for money to live. At least it was an honest living. In her present position, she offered her soul and in the future, her son would become part of the deal.

A pained cry escaped. If she had her life over, she'd do things differently.

A grunt came from behind, and she whirled to see a black cat loping after her. It skidded to a halt and rubbed against her legs.

The creature seemed to have taken a liking to her and followed her around all day.

If it weren't for Iseult, she might have tried to purchase the feline because her son would adore having a pet.

"Where have you been, kitty-cat?"

The creature lifted its head and stared at her with bright-green eyes. Her heart skipped a beat. Leo had green eyes of almost the exact shade.

She put on a burst of speed as if trying to outrun her turmoil. She'd dreamed of Leo yet again. A whoosh of heat bloomed in her face. Goddess. Her dreams still held the power to embarrass her and shove warmth to her cheeks.

They taunted her since she'd never have Leo in that manner.

Leo belonged to Iseult.

She came to her favorite spot and settled on the grassy patch that overlooked the beach and the rush of the green waves during the solar day. While she had picked at her dinner, darkness had fallen and strategic colored lights lit her way.

The cat sprawled beside her, seemingly content to doze while she tried to hide from her conscience.

Leo.

She hadn't seen him, although he had to be here somewhere. Tomorrow, she'd ask at reception, spin them a story about meeting him on Dalcon. Despite her abhorrence, the truth was she had no alternatives. Time to start her gruesome task. A sour taste in her mouth had her swallowing. Once. Twice. It did nothing to relieve the bitterness or halt the uneasy heaving in her belly.

Tomorrow, she'd attempt to sign up one of the Mitchell brothers. If they refused, she'd turn her attention to a male relative.

She stood abruptly and hurried to her bungalow, desperate to jump into the sanitizer to bathe the unclean sensation from her skin.

Then, once she was spotless, she'd take a potion so she could sleep throughout the night, undisturbed by the vivid dreams of Leo plunging into her receptive body.

Betrys flung open her door and let the big cat inside, since the creature seemed determined to enter. She slammed the door shut and unfastened the woven cream belt that secured her robe in place. Nimble fingers pulled the clips from her hair and let it topple down her back. She stepped out of her robe and left it in a heap on the tiled floor.

Purify. She needed to wash her skin to get rid of this itchiness. A pity she couldn't scrub her mind too.

"Water medium-hot." She stood in the sanitizer for ages, hot steam and a fine spray pounding her skin. Yet no matter how high she ordered the temperature, or how long she stood there, she couldn't seem to get clean.

Finally, she switched the unit to dry. Naked, she wandered to her sleep-bed. The cat rested on the end and lifted its head on her entry to the bedroom. Its green gaze seemed to drill inside her—her imagination working overtime for sure, but she gave an uneasy laugh.

"I bet you lead an uncomplicated life. Sleeping, eating and playing on the beach. I wish I were a cat like you, then I wouldn't be stuck in this impossible situation."

The cat's gaze followed her as she pulled a tonic from the storage drawer containing her few belongings.

After shaking the bottle, she opened it and drank the contents before pulling back the covers and crawling into the sleep-bed.

Blissful sleep, free of Leo dreams and thoughts of Iseult. Her wants were small.

Leo watched her toss and turn and gradually succumb to the liquid she'd drunk. An uncomplicated life. Huh, she'd tossed him into a hellish existence, one full of pain and nightmares.

He shifted and went to the door to retrieve the clothes and his com-circle he'd hidden before he'd gone to find her. His scar started to ache, and he massaged his stomach with his free hand.

"I'm ready, Saber. She's out. Drugged herself with some sort of sleeping tonic, which makes things easy for me." Leo stalked to the bed and poked her side with his finger, grunting when she didn't stir. "I doubt she'll surface for hours. Meet you at the shuttle." He disconnected the call and scooped Betrys off the bed. At the last minute, he grabbed the sheet. She wouldn't need clothes where they were going.

Five minutes later, he met Saber at the shuttle. He'd carried Betrys through the resort and not a single person had attempted to stop him. They thought it was a game or some sort of role-playing and smiled and wished him good luck.

"Is she still out?" Saber asked.

"Yeah. She hasn't stirred."

"Are you sure about this?"

"I haven't changed my mind."

Saber opened the shuttle door so Leo could strap Betrys into a seat. "I asked Scarlett to do some last-minute research on her. There was no information on the computer. Nothing except her place of residence and the fact she works for a woman called Iseult Orna."

Leo nodded.

"Is that it?" Saber demanded. "Doesn't that strike you as strange? Everyone has a history of some sort. Scarlett can find anything, yet not on this woman."

"It doesn't worry me."

"Do you know more about her?"

"No," Leo said.

Saber cursed before climbing into the pilot's seat. He waited for Leo to strap into the seat beside him. "Three nights. I'll ping your com-circle when I'm about to land to pick you up or you can contact me earlier if you change your mind."

"I won't change my mind." Not in a million years. The woman was getting off easy, but maybe after he'd finished with her she'd think twice before snaring another man in her trap. Soon she'd know the fear, the sense of helplessness, experience a taste of the pain that came with forced sex. And he'd make sure she knew the shame of experiencing pleasure in the encounter, despite willing it otherwise.

Reality wouldn't resemble his weird-ass dreams. His mind's method of coping with his ordeal, yet it didn't explain the way he woke afterward, feeling the throb of well-used muscles. He shoved the thought away, having no traction with stupid dreams. They meant nothing.

"I wasn't going to tell you much more about your destination, but Eva told me I should give you the basics."

"You listen to your wife?"

"I love her," Saber said, not rising to his taunt. "And she's wise beyond her years."

"All right. What's so incredible about this place? I know you and Eva sneak away there for privacy."

Saber grinned. "We have the best sex there."

Leo shot his brother a look of censure. "I don't want to hear about your sex life."

Saber's grin widened, and it took years off his face. While Leo wasn't happy with his life, it pleased him to see the pleasure Saber and Felix took in their mates.

"While the village appears uninhabited, it is in fact inhabited by an incorporeal race. They feed on sexual energy, and this fuel makes them visible if they wish. They're very appreciative of any efforts on our part to feed them and are generous in return."

"You're shittin' me."

Saber shook his head. "Not this time."

"So they watch you have sex and absorb the energy from the act?"

"That's what I said."

Leo eyed his brother, and although he grinned, he didn't swerve from the facts of his tale.

"Don't believe me? You'll see for yourself."

Leo sank into his own thoughts and stared out the shuttle window to the darkness of the land below.

"If you leave the ruins of the village for any reason, make sure you watch for those big birds. We haven't seen any near the village, but take precautions."

"I'm not gonna argue," Leo said. "Those birds are scary."

"There's the village to the right."

Leo glanced in the direction his brother pointed and frowned at the lights. "I thought you said it appears deserted."

"They always seem to sense our intention to visit and prepare for us." Saber landed the shuttle and waited while Leo retrieved Betrys. "I'll show you the way."

Leo carried Betrys with little trouble. She was a tiny thing and could do with more weight on her bones. Not that he cared. Their break together would be a one-off. The woman was probably frigid and nothing like the passionate woman who stalked his dreams.

Saber opened the door to a scruffy-looking building and stood aside for Leo to pass. Instantly, soft light filled the interior, and Leo gaped, almost dropping Betrys in his shock.

This was the room from his dreams.

"Does it always look this way?" he asked.

"No." Saber blinked and turned in a slow circle to take in the bright hues. "During our visits, the room is full of pale colors, yet it feels cozy. All this vivid color reminds me of a sultan's tent."

"Greetings, friend," a masculine yet musical voice said.

"Caspar, this is my brother, Leo." Saber grinned. "He's brought a friend with him and intends to stay for three nights."

"You are welcome, brother of Saber," the masculine voice replied. "We prosper under your care and thank you."

"You're welcome." Saber turned to Leo. "Three nights. I'll be back early on the fourth day to pick you up. If you need anything, contact me with your com-circle or ask your hosts for help. They are very hospitable, especially if you please them."

CHAPTER SEVEN

L eo set Betrys on a sleep-bed and waited until he heard Saber leave before he started to explore the room. Rooms, he discovered once he'd prowled the interior.

"You are troubled," a voice stated.

"Caspar?"

"It is I."

"I dreamed of this room," Leo said.

"We sense your needs and adjust the décor to suit each visitor."

"I dislike people rifling inside my head." He hated the idea of the room, his dreams of Betrys becoming common knowledge. For one, the colorful dreams were sick. What sort of man dreamed of the woman who'd ensnared him in a trap that felt like death? A man should dream of sexy blondes with big boobs, curvy hips and seductive smiles. Not a brown mouse who wore a robe.

A sharp pain in his midriff made Leo grunt and double over.

He massaged his belly, yet the pain—a sort of uncomfortable pressure—remained.

"You are in pain." Caspar's voice was closer now. "Lie on the floor."

Exactly what his shaky legs and buckling knees were urging him to do. Leo sucked in a breath and pushed his hand against the tender spot. His touch made the burning ache back off, and he continued rubbing.

"Let me see." An order, not a suggestion.

Leo felt a mild tingling, then the pain subsided. He drew in a harsh breath and released it.

"Interesting. You will find a tonic in the cool-box. You already have some in your bloodstream, and it's producing a kind of antibody to kill the infection. Take the tonic and sleep. On the morrow, you will feel better."

"Thank you." Leo half crawled to the cool-box and pulled out a small glass vial full of a cloudy liquid. He removed the stopper and sniffed the contents. It was the same as the tonic given to him by the one-eyed woman in the market. Well, it couldn't hurt. He tipped the vial against his lips and gulped the medicine. A bitter taste coated his tongue, trickled down his throat and repeated swallowing didn't rid it from his mouth. The stuff was nasty, but if it helped him sleep instead of snaring him in the middle of weird-ass dreams, he'd endure.

Leo set the vial on the counter and staggered to the bed. Betrys lay still, small whistles issuing from her throat. Leo sighed, exhaustion pressing on his shoulders like a bag of cattle feed. He stripped off his clothes and dropped onto the bed, asleep before his head made a dent in the pillow.

The dream—that cursed dream in that cursed colorful room—started before he could tear himself away. Betrys blinked at him, her features full of wonder.

"You're here."

"It wasn't my idea." Leo took pleasure in the way her face dimmed, and he tried to ignore the wash of guilt that followed. Her fault he was feeling this way. *Her fault.*

"I know," she said, and he saw she really did understand his reluctance.

"I can't stop thinking about you. I try to stop myself, tell myself I hate you, but I keep dreaming of us making love."

"I know, Leo. Do you think I like working for Iseult? I don't. I hate it, but I have no alternative."

"You could walk away."

"No, I can't." She turned, presenting him with her back.

A sharp sound, quickly muffled, pulled at him. A sob? Leo slid closer and slipped his arm around her waist. He tugged her against his chest, and she made the sound again. Fuck, she was crying, but her words didn't make sense. Why couldn't she walk away from her job?

He asked the question, heard her breath hitch seconds before she twisted in his arms and kissed him. Leo tried to pull back, but she gripped his shoulders, blunt fingernails digging into his muscles. Her tongue slid between his lips, and the energy to fight fled. Her lower body rocked against him, his cock reacting like a purring kitten. Refusal wasn't an option, not when he wanted to return her kiss. Not when he wanted to part her legs and plunge his dick into her tight pussy. Not when he wanted to possess. Dominate.

Later, they'd talk. Right now he wanted to fuck.

A groan slipped from him as he propelled her to the bed. Unable to help himself, he pushed her onto her back before he rose over her slender form. He noted her tears, and they twisted something inside him, pierced some of his irritation. He'd planned to make her pay for her part in his misery, yet here in his dream—their dream—revenge didn't seem to matter.

His mind fastened on the sex part of his payback plan—the

seduction and the lovemaking, the taking by force.

He wiped away a tear with the brush of his thumb then kissed her, crushing his lips against hers with an inward groan. This woman wasn't his type yet his cock kept exerting an opinion, leading him astray, making him deviate from the plan he'd formulated.

Big time.

He cupped her face and watched her brown eyes fog with hunger. The knowledge of her yearning kicked him in the gut. She had about as much resistance as he. None. Sighing, he caressed her lips with his, explored the recesses of her mouth. Her tongue tangled with his, and slow shivers of desire slipped down his spine. He deepened the kiss, devouring her softness until lack of oxygen drove him to lift his head.

She ran her fingers over his face and kissed his chin, his cheek, his neck. When a kiss landed on the fleshy part between his shoulder and neck, he growled. Her mouth on that spot lit a charge in him. Her touch arrowed straight to his dick and he went so hard he thought he might self-implode.

Her lips eased from his neck, and the sensation lessened, allowing him to think again. He'd heard Saber and Felix talk about the mating site and how crazy it made them if their mates touched that spot.

Nah, this was a dream.

She couldn't be his mate.

"Leo, what's wrong?"

"You're not my mate."

She laughed, the sound jagged and brittle as if she'd forced herself to react. "I have no idea what you're talking about. Too much talking is bad." She winked and reached for him, her hard and passionate kiss taking him by surprise.

Their noses bumped, but she corrected the angle and gentled the pressure, seducing the seducer and drawing him into her snare.

His mind shied from the thought, and for an instant, he stopped responding.

"Stop." She scowled, shaking him by the shoulders. "We're the ones in this bed, on this dreamscape. No one else. This is just for us."

"Why are we here? Do you know?"

"My people dream. It's a peculiarity of the Petros race. My race."

"But what is the purpose of the dreams?"

Betrys's scowl deepened. "They're meant to forecast the future."

Leo snorted his disbelief. "Maybe we dream together, but I can't see us ever getting together in real life. There's too much history between us. Too much betrayal."

Betrys sprang off the bed. "I want to wake up. Wake up, Betrys. Wake up now."

"You don't want to talk about how you tricked me into signing the contract with Iseult?"

"I told you. I had no choice."

"You keep saying that, but you don't go into detail. Give me a reason, Betrys. Tell me why you lured me into Iseult's web."

Wake up. Wake up. Wake up!

Betrys kept thinking the words, willed herself to leave the dreamscape, to avoid Leo's questions—the questions he didn't ask when they were awake.

Wake up.

Her consciousness expanded outward, and instead of finding herself in her small room at Spiderus Mansion, she rested in a luxurious room ablaze with color. Beside her, Leo thrashed in the throes of his dream or nightmare. She shot off the sleep-bed and stumbled to the door. She wrenched it open and plunged outside into the darkness, each of her breaths coming in hoarse gulps.

It was quieter here, the black intense and somehow smothering. A shiver rippled in a series of bumps across her skin, and she realized she was naked. Yet instead of retreating, she wrapped her arms around herself and found a comfortable spot to lean against the wall while she tried to work out where she was and if she was still on the dreamscape.

Difficult to tell. This was all so confusing.

The cold started to bring more discomfort and drove her inside. Her gaze shot to Leo. Yes, he was still present.

She pinched her own arm and winced. Next, she attempted to summon clothes. That didn't work either. On surveying the room, a comfy chair with a jewel-green robe tossed over the back snagged her attention.

A similar green to Leo's eyes.

This time, the soar of emotions, the sudden breathlessness, held a different tone and meaning. *No*, she couldn't think about Leo in that manner. This dream walking had to cease. Iseult had sent her here to find another man of Leo's ilk. Yet every second she thought of signing up another man, nausea swirled through her stomach. If Iseult ever learned Leo was alive...

Goddess, her mind was a boggy mire.

It came down to two awful alternatives—signing up another man and sentencing him to a death warrant, or her son. She'd kept choosing the same path all along—continuing to save her son—but now she second-guessed her decision.

Either way, the path was intolerable because she suspected she'd never rid herself of Iseult, and Ricci would *never* be safe.

She donned the robe and tied the sash around her waist, grateful for the warmth. A knot formed in her throat because she knew what she had to do, even if the decision rubbed her raw.

Save her son.

She pictured Ricci's face, her longing to see him almost overwhelming.

"Betrys?"

"What, Leo?" She snorted inwardly. That was her

question—how did she get here and why?

"Come back to bed."

"Why?"

"You wanted a capture experience. Sex is part of the package."

She jumped up and whirled to face him. He lounged on the big sleep-bed, the covers pooled at his groin.

"Captured?" The word whooshed up her throat and emerged with a squeak.

His brows arched. "Isn't that why you came to Middlemarch Resort?"

"No," she blurted before she realized silence would've been the better answer. Aghast, she stared at him, her insides quivering with apprehension. He'd ask questions now, grill her about things she couldn't discuss.

"Why then?"

She shook her head.

He stared back, his gaze slicing and dicing, probing.

Betrys didn't flinch, managed not to show her internal panic, her fears and doubts. *Her guilt.* While she kept her expression impassive, the emotions swirled with the violence of a storm and fought hard for release.

At last, he nodded and stretched out his hand. "Come back to bed. You paid for a capture experience, and that's what you'll get."

Despite her uncertainty, her treacherous legs took on a mind of their own and propelled her toward Leo.

"Take off your robe."

"This isn't a dream," she whispered.

"You've had dreams?" His voice was sharp and demanded a response. "Sex dreams?"

"Yes." She felt defiance march across her face, settle on her lips and lift her jaw.

"Wait, you said you're a dream walker. We discussed it tonight. You're from the planet Petros, and your race can communicate with others via dreams."

She hesitated, then nodded. "We use it as an instrument to foretell the future. Not that it did us much good. Our planet imploded during a war with a neighboring planet. Most of our people died since the leaders of Matros were determined to take over Petros because of our mineral resources."

"How did you escape?"

"Corrin, my husband, smuggled me on a freighter." She sank onto the sleep-bed, her legs no longer strong enough to hold her upright. "He promised to join me as soon as he could, but I heard later he died that day in an explosion at the main square. That was three solar years ago."

"I'm sorry. I know how it feels to lose people you love." Leo reached for her arm and tugged her nearer. "Why do you keep wearing your white robe? It makes you stand out in the market."

"I have no currency to buy clothes." Besides, people—men—seemed to trust her more if she wore a robe. It made her appear unthreatening, the lack of threat emphasized if she wore her long hair in a braid and waived face enhancements.

"But Iseult must pay you well?"

"Yes."

He frowned at her, then seemed to come to a decision. "Get under the covers where it's warm."

A new type of anxiety struck her then because she wanted to touch him, have him caress her in return. It had been so long since a male had touched her with love. So long.

"You don't like me."

"You don't have to like someone to fuck them."

His words struck with the force of a weapon, stealing her breath, stealing her will, and making her want to cry. Instead, she lifted her chin and forced herself to meet his gaze.

"Is that what you're going to do? Fuck me?"

"Yes. Would you like to run? Scream a little before I get started?"

"No." In their shared dreams, he'd felt something. He hadn't acted callously, and no matter what he said, she didn't believe he'd injure her. She'd seen him with his brothers, and while he acted reserved, she'd never believe him capable of inflicting pain on someone weaker. "Running would be pointless."

"So you agree to let me shove my cock inside you?"

His words crystallized an emotion—the truth—and she inhaled sharply.

"I'm lonely," she said bluntly. "It doesn't matter if you don't have feelings for me. It will be nice to have someone hold me."

"Very well, Betrys Torin." Leo spread his arms and waited, his expression expectant.

They stared at each other for a long moment, and she realized he expected her to move across the expanse of bed to join him. He wasn't going to pounce. He wasn't going to force her. He wasn't giving her the opportunity to accuse him of rape.

After a brief hesitation, longing and loneliness, the desire to have something for herself, drove her to close the distance between them. She pressed against his chest, and his body heat seared into her green robe. His masculine scent, familiar yet new, filled each breath.

"I think we'll lose the robe," he said.

"All right." Was that her? She sounded uncertain and shy yet she was a grown female with a child. "Yes," she stated with more assurance.

Leo chuckled, the noise sudden, a little rusty, a little surprising. He helped her disrobe and tossed the garment on the floor. Then they were chest to chest, skin to skin.

Betrys sighed as her breasts flattened against his pectoral muscles. Sharing the dreamscape with Leo had been one thing, but this...this was something extra.

The room smelled of fragrant spices and flowers. A touch of herbs emanated from Leo, and the scent of the sleep-bed coverings brought to mind solar shine and fine days. Not a trace of the pungent market smoke. Leo's touch seared her skin, leaving a wake of tingles as his hand drifted down her spine to settle on her bottom.

His casual exploration of her breasts and hips made her bold, and she started an investigation of her own. She ran her fingers over his biceps and gloried in his swift intake when she pinched his nipple.

"The men on Petros don't have nipples. I've been wanting to touch them," she confessed.

He cocked his head, curiosity blooming for her to see. "Are there any other differences between Earth males and those from Petros?"

"Our men aren't as big here." She ran light fingers across his muscled chest. "The Petros race are not warriors, which is why our neighbors defeated us with little effort."

"The Petros men are scrawny?"

"They are slight of frame," Betrys corrected with a frown. "Not weak. We are—were—a nation of inventors, and the dreamscape aided us in our field of expertise."

Ricci was already showing signs of following in the footsteps of his father in this respect. He pulled apart everything to see how it worked.

"What is the purpose of nipples on a male?"

Leo chuckled, his expression becoming more open. "They have no purpose. On some men, they're an erogenous zone. On me, for example." He grinned to display a set of sharp, white teeth. "I enjoy a woman touching me there." He guided her fingers to one flat disc, his green eyes offering a silent dare.

She stared, then blinked at his laugh. Who was this playful man? Emboldened by the lurking humor, she began to explore, paying attention to detail—his sculpted muscles, strong legs, broad shoulders, beautiful face. At every part she touched, she watched and learned him from his responses.

A quick pinch, a drift of fingers, a firm press—he savored them all. She graduated to kisses and nibbles, and his breathing deepened. She pushed him onto his back and straddled his hips for better access.

"Ride me," he said. "You want me. I can smell your need."

Betrys stilled.

"Is that another difference between me and the men you used to know, Betrys? You only had sex in one position?"

The sound of her name on his lips did something to her, caused waves of longing for a future she could never have. She'd loved Corrin with all her heart, and they'd experienced a good marriage by Petros standards. Yet she was discovering cultural differences that made her marriage seem lacking.

The teasing, the smiles, the talking, and now Leo was asking—no, telling—her to take what she needed, to take charge of their lovemaking.

"Do you want me to tell you what to do? Or I could take over. Make you participate." His silky voice held a distinct air of mockery.

"I know the mechanics."

"So put them into practice, Betrys."

Each time he said her name he gave it two defined syllables, and he delivered it in a derisive tone. Half of her wanted to run while the other part of her wanted to stand up to his challenge in a very unPetros-like way.

A capture fantasy, he'd suggested.

Fine. Her turn to taunt and tease and deliver what he thought impossible. No restraints. No, that would remind him too much of Iseult—the last thing either of them needed. A reminder of the enemy who hovered in the room.

Betrys took a deep breath, part of her noticing Leo's avid gaze on her breasts as they rose and fell. She centered her mind and locked away the garbage from her past. Then she built a mental shield to imprison her fears of the future, and once this barrier was complete, she turned her attention to Leo. Such a pretty man, his exceptional looks highlighted whenever he smiled. The curve of his mouth lightened the green of his eyes and invited her to share in an answering grin.

Sexy, sexy man.

And he was hers to play with for this stolen moment.

He blinked, angled his head a fraction. "You never smile."

"Neither do you."

"Touché. Are you going to do anything?"

"Yes—at my own pace."

His smile widened, and his muscles rippled when he shifted to a more comfortable position. "I'll settle back and wait then. Don't take too long because I might doze off."

Betrys pressed her lips together. *Right. She'd show him*. She placed her hand on his chest and scooted back until she straddled his upper thighs. His cock was long and hard and fascinating. A tremor shook her hand as she reached to touch, and a sound of amusement came from him. She ignored the rude male and started exploring. His body temperature seemed much higher than her people, and his shaft burned with heat when she wrapped her fingers around his girth.

She moved her hand up and down, and a groan escaped him. She allowed herself to glance up, shoot him a smile of confidence when she noticed he clutched the bedcovers.

Feminine pique satisfied, she went back to appeasing her curiosity. His skin was soft and as she teased the head, a bead of moisture appeared at his slit. She wiped it away. Another drop of pre-cum appeared, and she bent to lap it up. A muttered curse came from Leo, and on lifting her head, she met his gaze. Green, green eyes full of heat, and was that desire?

Without breaking their connection, she closed her lips around his tip and explored with her tongue. She sucked and took more of him inside her mouth. His cock seemed to pulse and thicken and the beads of moisture appeared more often.

Her discoveries had an effect on her too. Heat roared in swirls to settle in her quim. Wetness pooled between her thighs and she hummed around his cock. It had been so long, and this was so much better than the dreamscape. This was real, with more of the scents and sounds and textures their shared dreams couldn't duplicate.

She lifted her head and released him. Seconds later, she was guiding him inside her with none of the awkwardness she'd imagined. His shaft stretched her to the point of pain, and she rose a fraction before impaling herself again. Up and down, she moved. Up and down. Up and down. Each slide became easier, felt even better. She changed the angle of her rise and fall, seeking a fit to make her enjoyment bloom.

"Yes," Leo said, his voice guttural and unlike his normal tones.

Her pulse spiked at his encouragement, and she increased her tempo. The prickle of pleasure heightened. It started deep inside her when Leo's cock hit the perfect spot during her downslide. A delicious tickle of heat that expanded until she gasped aloud, the velvet tension growing and growing and growing. Another push and the tantalizing slide up. She slid a finger over her clit, massaging the swollen nub, and filled herself with Leo's cock again. The coil of energy in her lower abdomen expanded, and she rubbed a little harder, a little faster, the bolts of pleasure coalescing into one big explosion.

She sobbed out loud and wished the pleasurable sensations would go on forever since they were so, so good.

The sensations drifted away, leaving the sexy buzz of satisfaction. Her eyes popped open—funny she hadn't even remembered closing them—and she sought Leo's gaze.

"When is it my turn?" he asked.

Betrys wanted to grin at his polite tone, but instead she sniffed.

"You think you can do better, then show me your moves."

He moved so fast, she scarcely had time to blink before she found herself on her back, her legs splayed and Leo looming over her. "Is that a dare?"

"Um...yes?" Betrys had no idea where this flirty self was coming from. This wasn't her, but having sex with Leo wasn't normal for her either.

He gave her one of those grins that made her breath catch and placed his cock at her entrance. He filled her with one thrust, and the friction of the hard slide awakened her desire. Another thrust stirred her nerve endings to a salute, and at the warm, wet suction of his mouth around the tip of one breast, she groaned. Arousal curled and spiraled low in her abdomen.

"You've got moves," she whispered.

"I know, but you haven't seen anything yet." His grin stole her breath. The man was too handsome for his own good, even with the short hair.

She clutched his shoulders as he paid attention to her other breast, the pull of his mouth and the wander of his hands fueling her desire. He thrust and withdrew, each stroke slow and purposeful. Her breathing became ragged, the clawing tension driving her to distraction. Leo trailed a line of kisses and nibbles down her neck. When he reached the base of her throat and the fleshy part of her upper shoulder, he let out a raw and guttural groan. His hips pistoned into her in increased speed, and his cock filled her to capacity.

He was slamming into her now, and an intense burst of heat seared her. The familiar low pressure gathered, and seconds later, she exploded with another climax.

Her pleasured moan and the tiny spasms of her quim around his shaft seemed to be the signal he was waiting for. He growled, and she felt the splash of warmth deep in her channel as he propelled into orgasm.

For long moments, they clasped each other, heartbeats racing and the faint sheen of sweat coating their skin. Leo's body became a heavy weight, and she squirmed in silent protest. He lifted off her and flopped onto his back. At her attempt to move, to go to clean up, his arm shot out. He grasped her arm and repositioned her against his side.

"There's no need to rush off," he murmured. "It makes me feel cheap if my partner in crime wants to run off straight away."

"I wasn't trying to run," Betrys said, but she was lying, and she knew it. Their lovemaking had felt too close, too personal. Now she felt wrong-footed and unsure. An understatement. She was desperate to regroup because she had to think of some way of getting Iseult another man before the weekend.

CHAPTER EIGHT

Betrys forced herself to relax, and she must've done a decent job of it because Leo's breathing deepened. Despite being tired herself, her brain wouldn't stop jogging around her problems.

What was she going to do? If she were honest, there was one option open to her. She knew it, she kept coming back to it, even as her mind rejected the choice. She needed to find Iseult her next lover, and she couldn't take one of the men who worked in the resort because of the family vibe.

Leo—despite the odds—had managed to survive and had suffered enough.

She had to figure out some other way.

Leo turned onto his side, and she took the opportunity to escape. She snatched up the green robe and tiptoed until she was safely outside.

If only she could take her son and disappear, but Iseult was too clever for her, always one step ahead. She never let Betrys go out alone with Ricci. There was no chance for real quality time because her interactions with her son were monitored.

She walked over to a broken wall and sat on the cold stone. An intense longing to see her son and hold him filled her, the wave of pain so sharp she almost cried out. Instead, she screwed her eyes shut and swallowed hard. Crying wouldn't help.

"Mother?"

Now she was cracking up—her mind imagining her son's presence. Impossible since he was at Spiderus Mansion on Dalcon.

"Mother, why are you crying?"

Betrys blinked to clear her vision. "Ricci? Ricci, what are you doing here? How did you get here?"

Her son's somber face creased into a frown. He glanced to his left and his right. "I don't know. Where are we?"

"We're on the planet Tiraq," she said, her mind racing. She could take Ricci and leave. It would mean leaving her nest egg, but that was a small price to pay. "What have you been doing since I left?"

"Iseult is grumpy. She made me stay in my room." He frowned again. "Iseult doesn't look well. She's not pretty anymore."

A sliver of panic struck Betrys. "She hasn't hurt you?"

"No, I obeyed her orders like you told me to."

Betrys wrapped her arms around her son and fought to act normal despite her lack of understanding. "Good boy," she murmured against his straight brown hair.

"Mother, you're holding me too tight."

"I'm sorry, son." Betrys forced herself to relax her grip on Ricci.

"I'm hungry," her son said. "Do you have any food?"

They needed to go now, before Leo woke. She doubted the man would help them, not after what she'd done. She peered into the darkness. With no idea of their location and no food, she couldn't just leave. It was too dangerous, which left her no better off than she'd been before.

The door to the old cottage opened, and Leo stood in the illumination that spilled outside. "Betrys? Betrys, where are you? It's dangerous out here, woman."

"Who's he?" Ricci whispered. "He looks awful grouchy."

The overloud whisper carried on the night air, and Leo's gaze settled on them, hard and implacable.

"Who's the kid and where did he come from?" Leo asked.

"This is my son, Ricci."

Another dreamscape. It had to be. Somehow, she'd fallen asleep and hadn't realized. Maybe stress was getting to her. Maybe Leo wouldn't remember or he'd think the dream was crazy or maybe...

No, that wouldn't work. One of the things she enjoyed about him was his intelligence.

"Your son?" Leo stalked closer, and Betrys glared at him.

"Put on some clothes."

Leo glanced down and blinked, as if surprised by his nakedness. "Come inside," he said, his tone less belligerent. "It's cold out here, and the boy will catch a chill."

Betrys gave a curt nod, and Leo acknowledged her agreement by turning and striding back inside.

"Who is that, Mother?"

"That's Leo Mitchell. He's a...ah...a friend," she decided. "We have food inside, maybe even some of your favorites."

"Do you think there will be sweets?"

She held out her hand, and her son clasped her fingers and followed her into the old stone building. Outside, the dwelling appeared dilapidated and uninhabitable, while the interior was a direct contrast of stylish comfort. She wondered if the Mitchells had done this on purpose and decided they had. It made a perfect getaway.

"Would you like a hot drink?" Leo asked.

He was making it for her? She nodded in dumb shock and

watched him make a pot of the tea, the drink a lot of the resort guests drank. She'd never drunk the beverage until her visit to Ione Island.

"What about your son?"

"I want to drink what you're having," Ricci piped up.

Betrys frowned. "Will it hurt him?"

"No, my brothers and sister and I all drank tea from an early age. I'll make some ham and cheese sandwiches too."

Now Betrys stared harder. "You're doing women's work."

"Preparing food isn't a woman's job," Leo said, his hands busy as he spoke. "Who said it was? I'm hungry and enjoy eating. My mother taught all of us to cook. I'm a better cook than my sister."

"What's a sandwich?" Ricci asked. "Mother, is that an alien food?"

"On Petros, the women make food." Betrys placed her hand on her son's shoulder in a request for silence. "Our tasks are—were—distinct and defined so everyone knew their place."

"Not on Earth. Women undertake lots of jobs that used to be the male domain."

"I want to learn how to cook." Ricci's face was earnest as he stared at Leo—now wearing a green robe.

"What's your name?" Leo asked.

"My name is Ricci," her son said.

Leo shot her a look then studied her son. "Where do you live?"

"Spiderus Mansion." Ricci moved closer to Leo. "It's good there but I don't see Mother very much."

Leo cast her another quick glance, this one considering, and she could almost see his mind shuffling the facts Ricci had innocently leaked.

"Ricci, don't get in Leo's way." She spoke before he started to ask questions.

"He's not in the way."

"What is this stuff?" Ricci asked, his chatter and curiosity providing a barrier between her and Leo's questions.

"That's bread," Leo said. "You can help me make the sandwiches."

Betrys stood back and let Leo guide Ricci in the making of what Leo called toasted sandwiches. She'd never heard of them either, but Leo grabbed her attention as he interacted with her son. He didn't talk down to Ricci, didn't growl at him when her son became too enthusiastic and dropped fillings on the floor, didn't treat him as the enemy.

Leo handed her tea in a beautiful cup that sat on a matching saucer. "Go and sit. Relax. Ricci and I have this under control."

She found herself accepting the beverage and retreating—a sort of out-of-body experience.

"I thought you would enjoy interacting with your son," a masculine voice said.

Betrys started, her cup rattling on its saucer as she whirled to face the stranger. A tiny squeak escaped her before she registered the man's non-threatening manner.

"Don't worry. This is our host," Leo said. "He and his people are incorporeal and own the village." Leo returned to his task, his voice low while he spoke with her son.

"I'm sorry I scared you." The well-dressed man sprawled in a chair. Black trews encased his legs, and he wore a frilly white shirt. He reminded her of a sexually satiated male with his relaxed demeanor and his sleepy-eyed gaze. "I mean you no harm."

"Incorporeal?"

"Yes." His grin was languid and satisfied. "Your lovemaking with Leo tasted rather piquant. You have fed us well."

"Pardon?" She knew she was gaping, but she couldn't seem to stop herself. "I don't understand."

"My race feeds on sexual energy. Since the Mitchell family arrived on Ione we have fed more often. Our race is thriving again."

"Um, that's good," she said in understatement. She thought of what she and Leo had done together on the bed, and heat surged to her cheeks. They'd watched them have sex?

"You don't need to feel embarrassed," the man added with a broad smile. "Sex is a natural thing."

"Um, yes. What should I call you?"

"You can call me Caspar."

"My name is Betrys. How did Ricci get here? Did you have something to do with it? Am I dreaming?"

"Your son has the power to create dreamscapes, but he hasn't harnessed his talent yet. I aided his journey and escorted him here. As an incorporeal, I have to power to create illusions. I'm able to pluck wishes from minds and make them come true."

"So all of this," she made a sweeping motion with her hand, "isn't real."

"It's real enough. The items we conjure last for as long as the recipient requires them. That's the simplest explanation. We gift those who please us with our largesse."

Betrys thought about that for a moment and scowled. "So Ricci will disappear."

"When he wakes."

Ah, she knew his appearance was too easy, too convenient. "I wanted to see my son so much."

"I know," Caspar said, his smile fading. "You are in a difficult position. You should tell Leo. He is a good man, and despite appearances, he likes you."

Betrys glanced over at Leo, who was listening to something her son was saying. "I can't. No matter what I do, I'm stuck in Iseult's trap."

"Sharing a problem is a good way to find new alternatives."

"The sandwiches are ready," Ricci announced.

"Set them on..." Betrys glanced around for a suitable place and gasped when a table appeared out of thin air. "There."

"I must go. I will be back to guide Ricci through the dreamscape.

He will arrive back at Spiderus Mansion without any problems."

"Thank you," Betrys said.

Caspar smiled. "Love well." Seconds later, he and his chair disappeared.

"Leo promised we can have a special dessert after our sandwiches. He said it's a pav-pav—" He broke off and glanced at Leo. "What is it, Leo?"

The hero worship in her son brought a sting to the back of her eyes. She swallowed hard. Once. Twice. *Do not weep. Do not.*

Leo ruffled Ricci's hair. "A pavlova. It's my favorite dessert, and my mother always made one for my birthday every year. In my family, the birthday person always got to choose what they wanted to eat for their birthday meal. Of course, some years we'd have parties."

"I've never had a party before." Ricci's small face radiated excitement.

"It's an Earth custom," Leo explained. "Every planet does things in different ways."

"I don't remember Petros." Ricci accepted the plate Leo handed him and bit into a sandwich. "I like sandwiches."

"Glad to hear it." Leo handed a plate to her.

"Thank you." Betrys couldn't meet Leo's gaze. She knew he'd have questions, but she hesitated in the provision of answers.

"Tell me about Earth, please, Leo." Animation made Ricci's face glow, and it tugged at her heartstrings. Her one regret about her marriage—Corrin had always been busy with administration and organizing sales of their forecasting skills. That left few personal moments for their son. Now, he was reveling in Leo's attention.

Betrys listened to Leo's husky voice as he described the antics of his brothers and sister and their cousins. Much like her son, she listened enthralled, the corners of her mouth hitching upward as he spun tales of swimming in the river during the hot part of the year. He told them about his dog—an Earth creature—that had died at eighteen years old and left him heartbroken.

Ricci let out a sudden yawn, and a pang of disappointment struck her. Selfishly, she wanted to keep her son with her and enjoy his company for longer. The parent in her overruled her initial instinct. "It's time for you to go to sleep, my son."

The moment was bittersweet. Her normal interactions with her son were short, and she was aware the time spent with Ricci occurred because Iseult allowed the indulgence.

"Stretch out on the long chair," she said.

"Will you and Leo be here in the morning?"

Her son's innocent question pumped sorrow through her, and she was sure Leo caught the strain lurking under her smile. "I'll be home soon."

Ricci yawned again, and she hustled him to the long chair.

Leo followed her. "I'll tell you a story about my brothers when they were your age."

Betrys picked up a soft blanket off the end of the sleep-bed. She was sure it hadn't been there before and presumed Caspar had provided the blanket for her son. She hoped the incorporeal man kept his word and escorted Ricci safely back to his bed. Most Petros children received training and knew to leave a mental tie at their starting point, so they never wandered lost in the dreamscape. She hadn't passed her training on to Ricci because Corrin had tested him and declared he lacked the talent to forecast the future by dreams.

She'd have to rethink that because it was obvious Ricci possessed a little dream-walking talent—enough to put him in danger if left to his own devices.

Betrys worried about her new problem and let Leo's voice wash over her as he told Ricci a bedtime story. Maybe Caspar would know the extent of his power, or maybe...maybe the power came from the incorporeal man. Hope surged then dropped to the pit of her stomach. No, her son would need to have some sort of latent talent to make the journey in the first place.

Another problem to add to her load, because if Ricci mentioned his new experiences or meeting Leo to Iseult, the quagmire she stood on would turn to quicksand.

Two problems—Iseult would learn about Ricci's dream walking and connect the dots. She'd make the mental jump and come to the conclusion that Betrys held the same power as her son. Iseult would want to exploit the power to further her own ends, which led to the second problem. Iseult would learn Leo was alive, she'd discover Betrys had conspired to hide the truth from her, and she'd learn she couldn't trust Betrys to follow her orders.

Leo watched the child fall asleep but continued telling his story to give himself space to think. *Betrys has a son.*

Ricci's existence added all sorts of layers to his questions. Why did Betrys troll the Dalcon market for Iseult? Why did she continue working for the woman when it was obvious she hated her job? And why didn't she see much of her son? What hold did Iseult have over her that made Betrys follow the woman's orders?

The scar on his stomach was aching again, the pain becoming more intense by the second. He needed to drink another one of those tonics. They tasted disgusting but they did make him feel better once he'd choked down the foul mixture.

Betrys never stirred when he wandered to the kitchen area. He opened the cold-box and found another vial of the tonic. He pulled out the stopper, took a quick breath and guzzled the contents. For a few seconds he thought his stomach might revolt, but he swallowed hard three times and his gag reflex retreated. The pain also ceased, leaving him free to return to his questions.

"Why do you let Iseult keep you from your son?"

Betrys's head jerked up and she regarded him mutely.

"I'm waiting for an answer."

"I don't have to appease your curiosity."

"You made it my business by approaching me in the market." Leo stood, anger finding an outlet in clenched fists. "The way I see it is I can keep you here until you provide the answers I'm seeking."

"You can't do that. Iseult is expecting me back at Spiderus Mansion. I can't stay away for much longer. Please, Leo. Iseult might hurt Ricci if I don't return on schedule."

At seeing her distress, he took half a step toward her, his first instinct to comfort her, then he realized what he was doing and came to an abrupt halt. "Tell me why you're working for Iseult. What hold does she have over you?"

A tear spilled free, highlighting her misery, and Leo found himself standing in front of her. He hated her, he told himself. Yet it was inhuman to watch someone—no matter who or what they were—suffer. He wrapped his arms around her and pressed her face to his chest.

She started crying in earnest then. Fuck, had he changed so much that he'd wage his war against a woman? Betrys felt slight and fragile in his arms, yet he knew she bore an inner core of strength. She had to in order to survive.

When she stopped sobbing, he ran his hand down her back and put some space between them.

"If you don't give me answers, I can't help you," Leo said, scanning her face.

"Why would you want to help me after everything I've done?"

Her face was blotchy and her looks suffered from her crying jag. She never flirted or batted her lashes at him, and he kind of enjoyed her manner. Some people put a lot of stock in good looks. Some people treated him differently because the gene pool had worked in his favor. Some people were blind.

"Explain everything to me, and I'll make that decision."

Betrys tried to smile, tried to act nonchalant, tried to pretend everything was fine. She failed. Clammy sweat formed on her torso, between her breasts, and she started when Leo reached out and used a single finger to lift her chin. She blinked under his intense scrutiny, tried to glance away, but he wouldn't let her.

"Tell me the truth, Betrys. You're trying to protect your son. I get that. I do. But tell me the rest. Fill in the gaps for me."

Leo's tone straddled reasonable and persuasive. She wrapped her arms around her torso and tried to speak. All that emerged was a croak. How could Leo help? No one could save her and Ricci because she'd made mistake after mistake. She'd procured men for her boss in the knowledge they'd die. She was a murderer, or at the least an accomplice.

"Iseult will kill Ricci if I don't follow her orders." Unable to stand still, she started pacing in jerky steps. She came to an abrupt halt by the long chair and stared at her sleeping son. Leo moved to stand beside her, not touching, but so close she was aware of his body heat and his silent command for her to share details of her life in Iseult's household.

As she stared at her son, he started to fade. She gasped, and Leo wrapped an arm around her shoulders in silent comfort. Caspar had promised he'd look after Ricci, but she couldn't help but worry. She'd received a little basic training and knew of the dreamscape, almost from the moment of her birth. Every Petros child held the same understanding, even if the skill never materialized, and the instant her talent had propelled her onto the dreamscape, her instincts had taken over, and she'd known how to control her power. Ricci possessed none of that vital knowledge.

Once Ricci had faded away to leave nothing on the long chair apart from the soft blanket that had covered him, a ragged sob emerged. Without knowing how it happened, she found herself wrapped in Leo's arms while she wept.

Control.

She'd never possessed influence over her path in life. First her parents, then her husband, had governed her actions and kept her secure. Coping on her own wasn't easy, but she'd done her best. She hadn't wanted to rely on anyone else for her happiness, not since she was capable of doing the job. With independence her goal, she was failing badly.

Leo grasped her shoulders and shook her to grab her attention. "Stop this crying. Come." He tugged on her hand, and she stumbled after him. He unfastened the tie on her robe and had her naked in seconds. Before she could protest, he scooped her off her feet and set her on the sleep-bed.

Seconds later, Leo joined her and pulled her into his arms. "Tell me everything. How did you come to work for Iseult, and why did you come to the resort now and leave your son at Spiderus Mansion?"

Leo couldn't help her, but maybe talking about her problems would present a solution. She started at the beginning. "Corrin, my husband, must've suspected something was wrong. He told me to gather our belongings and he'd join us later. He never came. I arrived on Dalcon and wasn't sure what to do. I decided to stay in a hotel and wait for Corrin. When he didn't arrive, I knew he'd died. I started to hear rumors about the downfall of our people and knew I had to find a job because my resources were low. There aren't many positions available for a woman with a child. I needed to find a place for us to live, and the job with Iseult for an assistant seemed perfect."

"But it wasn't."

"At the start, I took care of administration tasks, the ordering of food supplies and making sure the mansion was clean and tidy. Then, once I'd settled in, Iseult called me to her web and gave me instructions to procure a man for her."

"Why didn't you leave at that point?"

"I refused and said I would leave. Iseult said if I tried to leave, she would order my son killed."

"You believed her."

"Oh yes. Iseult never offers empty threats. If she says she will do something, she always follows through. Yes, she meant to kill Ricci."

"So why are you here at the resort?"

"Iseult enjoyed you so much, she decided I should travel to your home planet and find a relative for her. She intends to pay well, but it's a death sentence."

"I didn't die," Leo said.

"I know, and I don't understand why you survived. Iseult has changed since she...ah..."

"Since she abused me," Leo said.

Betrys winced at his bluntness. "Yes. She can't hold her humanoid form. Her face remains the same, but she can't control her shape. Her legs and torso remain in spider form most of the time."

"So if you turn up on Dalcon without a man for Iseult, she will kill Ricci?"

"Yes, she has promised this."

"We'll come up with a plan to save Ricci, but first I want you to contact Iseult and tell her you're having difficulty in getting a man to agree to your proposition."

"But she won't settle for that. She expects a successful outcome to my journey."

Leo fell silent, and Betrys thought he realized the futility of going against Iseult. Somehow, she had to talk a man into signing Iseult's contract.

It was the only way.

"Tell her that the men here are very well paid, and you think you might be able to get one to sign the contract if you have permission to increase your remuneration offer. Ask her for another solar week in which to negotiate with the local men."

"That might work, but what is the point of prolonging things? The end result will be the same. Iseult still has Ricci, and while she has my son, I'm powerless to disobey her orders."

"The delay will give us a chance to formulate a plan. We'll tell my brothers, and together we'll work out a strategy to retrieve Ricci from Spiderus Mansion. Once we have your son safe, Iseult will lose her hold over you. She can't force you to follow her orders."

"She can still kill me."

Leo leaned over and smiled at her. "She won't kill you. She has to get by me first."

"I don't understand. Why would you help me? Protect me?" The events of her past returned in a surge of horror, vibrant in their intensity. Self-loathing hit her over the head, and her brain scrambled to make sense of Leo's behavior. Why? Why would he treat her as a friend when she'd exploited him for her own ends?

"You made sure I got home to my family. You're doing your best to keep your son safe. And I've come to like you a little bit."

"Oh."

Leo flashed a grin, so bright it caused her to blink. "Is that all you can say? You usually have a lot more to say for yourself. I remember meeting in the market, and how persuasive you were, how fast you talked to convince me to sign Iseult's contract."

"That was fear. A person can do a lot of things they wouldn't otherwise do if they're driven by fear."

"We can't do anything else tonight," Leo said. "But tomorrow, we'll contact Saber and get him to collect us."

"You think we can get Ricci?"

"I know it," Leo said, and he dropped a kiss on her lips. "But since we're stuck here with nothing much to do, I have a suggestion of a way to occupy ourselves and thank our hosts for bringing Ricci to visit."

"You do?"

"You have a good kid there, Betrys. A son to be proud of."

Pride filled her for a fleeting second before she recalled her situation, their situation. "You're in just as much danger as Ricci.

If Iseult discovers you're still alive and I let you leave Spiderus Mansion, she won't rest until she has you again."

"Iseult is not going to touch me again," Leo said, kissing her to halt their conversation. He took the kiss deeper and feasted on her mouth until a rough growl vibrated in his chest.

Betrys resisted at first but was no match for Leo's determined seduction. He wedged her thighs apart while he skated his thumb along the outer curve of one breast. Hot pleasure spilled into her with each of his erotic touches, and soon she floated in blissful comfort.

"Leo," she whispered.

"Tell me what you want."

"I want you inside me. Please, Leo."

"The perfect answer." He moved farther down her body, his fingers branding every inch of her flesh with his touch. The muscles of her stomach flexed under his explorations, and the second he grazed the sensitive nub hidden in her folds, she let out a moan.

"Leo, please take me now."

He grinned. "Nothing I'd enjoy more."

In seconds, he rose over her, positioned his cock and slid deep. He filled her with his male strength and his hard length. When he started moving, it was magical, the bliss more than the previous occasion. It was as if her confession had lightened her spirit and given her permission to relax.

She sought his mouth and kissed him, putting everything she felt into her caress. The passion. The pleasure. The enjoyment of losing herself in a man.

Higher and higher, he drove her, and with a snap of tension, she fell into ecstasy, the pulses shooting through her body sheer indulgence.

Leo must have felt her climax because he stroked into her with three hard thrusts then stilled, his breath coming in harsh gasps.

After long moments, he separated their bodies and drew her against his chest.

"That is a much better way to use our time," he purred in her ear.

"Yes," she whispered in agreement, but a worrying thought settled in her mind. Why would Leo want to involve himself in her problems? By the Goddess, she needed to read her cards to find her way.

CHAPTER NINE

Iseult scrambled along the white passage leading to her central web, her eight legs working in concert for a change. The vibrant colors remained on her torso, but she still couldn't maintain the humanoid form—not with her usual competence.

Ever since the last man.

Yes, since she'd taken Pretty she'd been off kilter, the drunken euphoria that engulfed her leading her to space out and lose moments of reality.

"You," she snapped at one of her guards.

"Yes, lady?"

"I want to speak to all the guards who tasted the man's blood. Tell them to assemble in my web. I await their arrival."

"Yes, lady."

She paused to watch the guard scuttle away. Strong legs, she mused. Curvaceous and pleasing torso. Perhaps she should add him to the breeding roster. It never hurt to have spares on her list since she was a vigorous lover.

Iseult inhaled to center herself and visualized her other form. The familiar tingles of transformation brought a sense of satisfaction. She was becoming stronger again, yet still, unease lurked in her mind. Something was wrong, something odd that her ingrained awareness failed to acknowledge.

Her mouth twisted as she took a mental trip to the past. The females of their species didn't play nice together, and on reaching sexual maturity, they left to set up on their own. Everything was instinctual, but in this case, she was coming up with nothing. Not one of her innate senses was helping to choose one path over another.

Instead emptiness filled her, a sense of loss, and she had no idea of what she'd misplaced.

Leo woke at his usual time. Early. He didn't move, didn't so much as twitch a muscle. One moment he was asleep, then he was wide awake and staring at Betrys.

She wasn't beautiful, yet her strength of character attracted his attention. His cock stirred, exerting a say on his thoughts. Oh yeah. He enjoyed her body too. He liked the way her smile lit up her face, and he'd witnessed firsthand her love for her son. He'd seen the helplessness on her face as she'd spoken of her situation, her desperate need to protect Ricci and keep him safe. Despite the danger to herself and her son, she'd helped him leave Spiderus Mansion. She'd said if Iseult had discovered he was alive, she would've kept him at the mansion. Leo was inclined to believe Betrys's supposition.

Yeah, gradually he'd changed his mind about her, coming to

admire her without knowing how or why regarding his difference of opinion. Despite his words to Saber, he'd stopped yearning for revenge and started to wonder why Betrys was working for Iseult.

Now he had his answers.

The problem was how to deal with Iseult.

He slid from the bed, and Betrys murmured a sleepy protest. Leo ambled to the kitchen area and wondered about coffee. No sooner had the thought occurred than a coffeemaker appeared, prepped and ready to go. While he blinked, water started dripping through, and the scent of coffee filled the air.

"Score," Leo said, and a rich chuckle sounded in the corner of the room. Leo grinned and found a mug to stick beneath the flow of coffee. With a coffee in hand, he grabbed his com-circle and wandered outside to call Saber.

"Bro," he said when Saber answered.

"You sound happy."

"Yeah. I've met Caspar in person. Top man. Thanks to him, I know way more about Betrys." He told his brother about Betrys, her son and her employer Iseult.

"Ah, I knew there was more to the story than you told us. Iseult Orna, her employer, right?"

"Yeah. That's the one."

"She's booked in for the next intake at the resort," Saber said in a cool voice. "She wants to bring six guards with her."

"We don't want her here or her minions," Leo snapped. "She's dangerous, and any man she fucks will die. Betrys says they all perish, that I'm an oddity in this respect."

"Betrys doesn't know why you lived?"

"She has no idea. Apparently, it's never happened in all the time she's worked for Iseult."

"If we let Iseult come to the resort that might open an opportunity for us to snatch Ricci while she's not at home."

"Betrys can't go," Leo said, thinking aloud. "She'd need to stay here and let Iseult think she's searching for another male. The woman is dangerous, Saber. We need to have a solid plan in place. We can't risk any of the men or let Iseult get her hooks into them. She'll kill them. Saber, she'll abuse and torture them. We can't let that happen to anyone else."

"Steady, Leo. We're not going to let her touch anyone. We'll drug her if we have to and keep her subdued. Betrys will know her favorite foods. Don't worry. We'll talk to Betrys and formulate a plan to keep her and her son safe. And if what Betrys says is true, we need to keep you out of sight. You'll need to stay in feline form for the duration of Iseult's stay or at least until we're able to make sure Betrys's son is clear of danger."

Saber's calmness soothed some of the angst riding Leo. He set his empty coffee mug aside and rubbed at the scar on his belly. The damn thing was throbbing again and it made him even more determined to best Iseult.

"Leo, you said Iseult is having trouble keeping her form. If we give her something to make her sick or incapacitate her, she might think the illness is another mysterious symptom."

"That might work. I'll talk to Betrys. Maybe she has other info we can use. Will you come and pick us up today?"

"No," Saber said after a pause. "I'll come and collect you tomorrow. It's not as if we can do much today, not before we do some research. I'll get Scarlett on the job. She'll obtain the information we need, but it will take time."

Leo nodded, even though his brother couldn't see him. Spending more hours with Betrys wasn't a hardship. "All right. I'll contact you if Betrys can think of anything else that might help us."

"Right. I'll be there around mid-morning. Tell Betrys not to worry. We'll get her son."

"Thanks," Leo said.

"Anytime," Saber replied and cut the connection.

Leo idly rubbed at his scar, his touch easing the ache. He frowned and looked down at his naked form. Either he was putting on weight or there was something wrong with his stomach. He should be getting better, the pain lessening rather than increasing.

"Take more of the tonic," Caspar said from the doorway.

"Do you know what is wrong with me?" Leo asked, turning toward the familiar voice.

"I am no medical man, but I suspect you've picked up a parasite. It happens. The tonic will help to kill off the organism."

"Crap." An understatement. Leo scowled at his puckered scar and prodded the swelling. More questions for Betrys and more research for Scarlett.

Caspar smiled. "I like young Ricci. Betrys has an intelligent son. He was full of questions during the journey back to his sleeping body."

"Most children are curious," Leo said. "I remember my younger brothers asking questions, and I'm sure I asked my share."

"There are more of you?" Caspar asked in clear interest.

"I have four brothers and one sister," Leo said.

Caspar's grin held joy and expectation. He rubbed his hands together. "I can't wait to meet the others. Do they have mates?"

"Not all of us. Saber and my second brother Felix have mates."

"I've met Saber and the beautiful Eva. Perhaps your siblings could come to visit." Caspar peppered him with more questions.

Leo answered Caspar's queries until Caspar halted him.

"Betrys is awake," Caspar said. "I will inform her that I escorted Ricci home, then leave you in peace."

The man *poofed* out of sight, and Leo ambled back inside to grab more tonic and start making breakfast.

"Good morning," he called.

Betrys looked adorably flustered, and his heart did a flip-flop, sort of like a landed trout. The thought made him smile. The more he learned of Betrys, the more he overcame his lingering dislike of her actions.

"I'll make breakfast. What would you like?"

"I'm hungry," she announced, her tone loaded with surprise. "I don't have a chance to break my fast at the mansion. Iseult keeps me busy."

"Caspar tells me I have some sort of parasite, which is why my scar is giving me so much trouble. Do you know if this has happened before?"

"You think this came from Iseult?" Betrys slid off the sleep-bed, glanced around for a robe. "Let me see."

Leo stood still while she ran gentle fingers over the scar.

She glanced up at him. "Does it hurt if I push on it?"

Leo sucked in a harsh gasp and stepped from her reach.

Betrys frowned. "I'm sorry. I didn't mean to hurt you. The area looks swollen."

Leo opened the cold-box and grabbed a vial. He removed the stopper and knocked back the liquid inside. "This tonic seems to relieve the pain, and the swelling subsides, for a while at least."

"Can I touch you again? I'll try not to hurt you. I promise."

Leo dipped his head in assent and steeled himself for Betrys's caress.

"Something is moving under there."

"Great," Leo said. "Caspar, is there something I can take to kill it?"

Caspar materialized beside Betrys, and Leo saw her start at the suddenness of the man's appearance. "If the parasite was in your digestive tract, I could help, but since it seems to be embedded in your flesh, someone will have to cut it out." He waved a hand and a display of knives—both plain and ceremonial appeared on the wall. "Take one of those. They should do the job."

"Iseult did this to me." Leo ignored Caspar's suggestion.

Betrys took an involuntary step back, regret and guilt chasing across her features. "It's never happened before. I don't know what to tell you. Everyone else died."

"Maybe Scarlett will turn up something in her research," Leo said. "I talked to Saber. Iseult has made enquiries about booking in at the resort."

"But she seldom leaves the mansion. I think she's attended two parties since I started working for her. She hired me because she doesn't leave Spiderus Mansion. Her men never leave either."

"From what Saber told me, it sounds as if she wants to bring six of her men too."

"That's out of character," Betrys said. "I wonder if she's tried to contact me."

"Saber never mentioned anything."

"She would've called my personal com-circle. It's in my room at the resort."

"Will she hurt Ricci if she can't contact you?"

"I don't know."

Leo pulled out his communicator and called Saber.

"Bro, it's me again. You need to go to Betrys's room and check her com-circle. We need to know if Iseult has tried to contact her."

"I'll get back to you," Saber said.

A sudden, sharp pain drove Leo to his knees. He clutched his stomach, his hands pressing against his scar.

"Leo." Betrys crouched beside him.

"Shift forms," Caspar said in a sharp voice. "Stand back, Betrys. Give him room."

The agony came again, sharp and breath-stealing. He groaned and pressed against the scar in the hope of pushing back the torture. His flesh rippled beneath his touch.

"Shift forms," Caspar barked at him like a drill sergeant. "Basics, son. Picture the cat now. Do it."

Leo pictured the cat in his mind, focused on it hard instead of the pain radiating from his middle. Cat. Cat. Black cat. Part of him was aware of the transformation beginning. He heard a cry from

Betrys, stifled when Caspar snapped a command. He struggled to hold the cat in his mind, struggled to focus, struggled to complete the change.

"Keep going, Leo."

Caspar's calm voice was a beacon. He focused on each instruction and willed his mind and body farther into the shift. He reached the point of no return and relaxed a fraction, knowing instinct would do the rest. A long moment later, he crouched in feline form, harsh pants rasping up his throat.

"Here, drink some water, lad." Caspar waved a hand and a bowl of water appeared beside him.

"He...you...oh my goddess," Betrys muttered.

Leo was too exhausted to bark out a laugh. He lapped at the water, just thankful the excruciating pain had subsided enough for him to think.

His com-circle buzzed.

"You'd better answer that," Caspar said to Betrys.

Leo couldn't have changed back if he'd wanted, not with his limbs shaky and weak.

"Hello, this is Betrys. Leo's stomach is giving him trouble. Caspar says he has a parasite and it needs to be cut out. No, you can't talk to him. He...he...he changed into a black cat. He can't talk. No, no he seems better now. Yes, I think you should come and collect us. Leo needs help."

"Tell Saber, I cannot aid Leo," Caspar said.

Leo heard Betrys relay Caspar's words.

She paused and nodded. "We'll be ready for you." She ended the call. "Felix and Casey are coming to collect us. Casey has a little medical training and has seen this happen to one of her men."

Leo growled in acknowledgement, too exhausted to move. This wasn't the way he wanted to expose his other self to Betrys.

Betrys gaped at the black cat. At Leo. No other word for it because her mouth was hanging wide open.

"I take it you didn't know," Caspar said, his rich voice full of amusement at her expense.

"He followed me around from the moment I arrived at the resort. I scratched him behind the ears and told him he was beautiful. I...I rubbed his belly!"

Caspar chuckled. "I'm sure he appreciated you running your hands over him. Don't fear, lass. The boy is fine. The parasite doesn't appear to enjoy him in his feline form. He hasn't hurt you, has he? At least that wasn't the terrified screaming I heard earlier, and my appetite is satiated."

Betrys lifted her chin, despite the embarrassment heating her cheeks. "You, sir, are not a gentleman."

Caspar laughed again. "My race are voyeurs, and I don't intend to apologize for our foibles. You should try it some time. The erotic sights are most invigorating."

Aware of Leo's gaze on her, Betrys crouched beside him and ran her hand over his silky black coat. "You are beautiful," she whispered. "How are you doing? Do you feel a little better? Can I see your scar?"

He flipped over onto his back in acquiescence and displayed his belly. Betrys drew in a swift breath. The scar bulged and...and it moved.

"Can I touch it?" she asked, deciding the best path was to request permission.

When he didn't offer an objection, she reached out and placed her hand on top of the bulge. It pulsed under the press of her fingers.

"Can you feel something in there?" Caspar asked.

"Yes, it's moving, although it doesn't seem as vigorous. I don't understand. It's obvious Iseult has done something to you, but this has never happened before. Leo, are you still in pain? Grunt once for yes, twice for no."

Leo let out three gruff barks.

Betrys wrinkled her nose. "What does that mean?"

Caspar chuckled, and Betrys shot him a glare.

"I think he means that it still hurts, but he's more comfortable in feline form," the irritating man said.

"Leo?"

Leo grunted.

"Okay then. I'd better tidy up before Leo's brother arrives to take us back to the resort."

"Have something to eat." Caspar gestured toward the cold-box and the kitchen area. "My people will take care of cleaning up."

"Thank you for letting us stay here," Betrys said. "I'm thankful for you bringing my son on the dreamscape to visit and returning him safely to the mansion."

"Lass, the pleasure is all mine. You can thank me by visiting again with your young man."

Betrys shot Leo a quick look and saw him resting, his head relaxed on his front paws. "I don't think Leo feels that way about me," she said in a soft voice. "I think this is a casual thing between us."

Leo lifted his head and grunted twice.

Caspar grinned in his annoying way. "Maybe the two of you should discuss the matter so you present a united front."

Betrys stood beside Caspar and Leo and watched the shuttle land. A dark-haired man jumped out, and a tall, slender woman with short black hair leaped out behind him, landing lightly on her feet. He nodded in acknowledgement of her and Caspar then focused on Leo.

"Leo," the man said and crouched beside his brother. "How are you doing?"

Betrys studied the new arrival and would have picked him as one of Leo's siblings or a relation. They possessed identical black hair and bright-green eyes, and they both moved with the same lazy confidence.

"You must be Betrys," the woman said. "I'm Casey, Felix's mate. Hi, you must be Caspar. You're looking very well."

"Thanks to the Mitchells, all my friends and family are doing well," Caspar said.

"Do you think you can help him?" Guilt was knocking Betrys over the head, and emotions swamped her without warning. She inhaled in an effort to regain her equilibrium. "This is my fault."

Leo growled in two distinct sounds.

"It is, Leo. If I hadn't approached you in the market..." Her shoulders rounded into a hunch. If it hadn't been Leo, she would've signed another willing male.

"Assigning blame won't help," Felix said, straightening from his crouch. "Let's load up and get back to the resort. Fingers crossed Scarlett has discovered information to help Leo."

Leo struggled to his feet and padded onto the shuttle. Betrys glanced at her clenched hands and noticed she still wore the green robe she'd found by the sleep-bed. She let out a squawk. "Wait, I need to get dressed."

Caspar bowed in her direction. "Wear it back to the resort, my dear. The robe will remain solid until you reach your room."

Betrys's eyes widened. "I think I might grab my own robe." She ran back into the dwelling and let out a squeak of alarm when Caspar appeared in front of her. She glared at him until he turned his back, and only then did she scramble into her own garments. "Thank you."

Caspar beamed. "My pleasure." He paused, then frowned. "Take one of my knives for your protection. A strong and admirable woman should receive gifts." He strode to the collection of weapons and selected a knife with a glowing ruby in the hilt. He pulled it from its leather sheath, studied the blade and replaced it. "Think of me whenever you use it."

"I couldn't."

"A mere token of thanks," Caspar said in a firm voice.

"Thanks." She stuffed the jeweled dagger out of sight in her pocket. "It was very nice to meet you, even if you do poke your nose into other people's private business."

Caspar's delighted chuckle followed her from the dwelling.

CHAPTER TEN

T he instant the shuttle landed at the resort, Felix, Leo, and Casey jumped out. Betrys shadowed them while wondering if she should follow or make herself scarce.

Leo halted and turned, his tail swishing.

"Leo, what—" Felix broke off, his gaze connecting with hers.

Betrys came to a complete halt at Felix's expression. There was worry and concern for his brother, and a fierceness that made her fear for her safety.

Leo growled low in his throat, and Felix severed their connection.

"Come with us," Casey said.

"No, I don't think—"

At Leo's sharp grumble, she stopped her verbal thought.

"Come with us," Felix ordered. "We'll need to ask you questions about Iseult. We need to know what we're dealing with." On uttering those words, he stalked off. Casey fell in behind, but Leo didn't move. At her hesitation, he padded up to her and gave the back of her legs a hard shunt in the direction his brother and sister-in-law had taken.

"Okay." Betrys sighed. Meeting the rest of his family felt like an ordeal, one she'd love to dodge. Another sigh whooshed from her. Hiding wasn't an option.

Felix and Casey disappeared inside a building.

"Where's Leo?" a masculine voice demanded.

"He's coming," Felix said.

Leo waited until she entered, then followed on her heels. The interior was spacious, yet Betrys found it difficult to discern the use of the space. An exercise area or perhaps another holo room. A sturdy table stood in the middle. Stacks of building materials and tins of paint filled the far corner. A work-in-progress, she decided.

"Betrys," the man said. "I'm Saber."

"Yes." She shifted her weight from foot to foot, trepidation doing a number on her nerves. After a hasty breath, she forced a smile. "You did the welcoming speech."

He gave a curt nod before turning his attention to Leo. "Scarlett hasn't discovered much. It seems the Spiderus race is secretive. We're going to need to make a decision. Do you want us to cut this thing out?"

"Bearing in mind the task might be beyond my skills," Casey declared.

"But if it's a parasite of some type, it would need to come out whenever it's finished its pupa stage or whatever the hell it's doing inside you." Felix added his opinion, and it wasn't difficult to discern his worry.

"He's in a lot of pain," Betrys said. "Caspar gave him a tonic, which helped a little. I've noticed him pressing on the wound, but I didn't realize it was bothering him so much. Almost overnight, the area has bulged out, and I could feel something moving beneath the flesh." Emotion built, became a heavy weight expanding up her throat, and she had to stop, swallow.

Leo moved closer and leaned against her legs. He butted her hand with his head and a choked laugh escaped her.

"You're not meant to comfort me." Her hand slid over his silky head, and she found herself scratching behind his ears. "This is my fault."

"Your fault?" Saber said in a sharp voice. "How so?"

Leo growled—a low and mean don't-mess-with-me snarl—and his older brother lifted both his hands in silent surrender. Then Leo butted her hand in a demand for more petting.

A shaky laugh escaped Betrys. "I guess Leo hasn't told you everything."

"You were the one who got him on the shuttle and sent him home when he was sick," Saber said. "For that, you have our thanks. Leo told us you have a son who is living at Spiderus Mansion. If I had a son, I'd want to protect him. I'd do anything to keep him safe. *Anything*."

"Thank you for understanding." Some of the tension leached from her muscles, and her hand resumed the slow up-and-down stroke of Leo's silky head. He leaned into her a little more, and a rumbly purr emerged from his throat.

Two more people arrived—another dark-haired man who resembled Leo and Felix, plus a young woman who wore her hair piled on top of her head in a donut-shaped bun. Her green eyes and black hair spoke of her relationship to the Mitchell brothers.

"Scarlett," Saber said. "Did you learn anything?"

She shook her head. "Nothing more than we already know. We're going to have to operate on instinct."

"I brought the instruments you wanted, Casey," the man said.

"Thanks, Sly." Casey accepted a black leather bag from a man who Betrys decided looked like another Mitchell brother. He possessed the same green eyes and black hair, long in his case, and held back with a hunter-green bandanna.

"Leo, let me see your scar." Saber took charge.

Leo obediently flopped over on his back to expose his stomach.

Betrys studied the scar along with the others. While it was visible, the old wound had lost its redness, and the swelling had reduced. "Something about his feline shape seems to make the thing inside him subside. If he's in humanoid form, the thing bulges out and pulses a lot more." She paused to take a breath, part of her surprised at her calmness. The man she'd touched and kissed possessed a dual nature. She'd had no idea and Iseult hadn't suspected a thing either. Maybe his feline characteristics had been the difference that saved him from death.

"Leo needs to shift to human," Casey said. "If what Betrys says is true, that would make the thing easier to cut out."

"We need a container to put the thing inside." Saber's creased brow told Betrys he was trying to think ahead and plan for contingencies. "Something solid that will keep it enclosed. Whatever it is, we don't want it to escape and find another host."

"What about a preserving jar?" Sly asked.

"Just the thing." Saber nodded in approval as Sly disappeared out the door. "Casey, get everything prepared and sterilized, ready to go before Leo shifts. We want him as comfortable as possible."

Betrys squeezed into a corner and acted invisible, clammy hands wrapped around her middle while she attempted to tamp down her growing panic. They were cutting Leo open—a dangerous act—yet the brothers and sister and Casey worked as a calm, competent team while she was the interloper. When she realized she was swaying, she placed one palm on the wall. Goddess, she hoped Leo survived this ordeal. Iseult hadn't done this to any other male. Was this a coincidence? Had his wound become infected since his return to the resort?

Sly rushed back, a preserving jar in hand. "I told Ma one of the beasts had a parasite, and we wanted a container so we could transport it to Dalcon for identification. She gave me a bottle of vinegar and said we should pour it over the parasite to preserve it."

Saber chuckled. "Did she want to come and watch?"

"She'd just put a batch of scones in the cook-box," Sly said. "She needed to supervise the new staff."

Casey pulled several items from the medical bag. "Place a clean sheet over the table. I'm going to inject the surface area with a numbing agent. The medical wand should do the trick. It might even spit out a diagnosis if we're lucky."

Saber walked over to Casey and Leo. "Okay, Leo. We're ready for you. Shift now, and we'll see what we've got."

Leo scanned the interior until he saw her trying to hide. He butted her leg with his head, and Betrys crouched to bury her head against his shoulder. The second she released him, he licked her cheek, the abrasive nature of his tongue across her skin transmitting messages of instant lust. A soft hum escaped her, echoed milliseconds later by a rumble that translated as satisfaction. Color rushed to her cheeks, and one of the brothers laughed. The heat in her face intensified.

"Save that for later, Leo," Saber said in a stern voice, but Betrys caught the underlying humor beneath his severity.

Casey sanitized her hands. "Let's do this."

Leo prowled toward the sheet-draped table. He stopped beside Saber, and his sigh was loud in the silent room. He didn't want to do this, and Betrys couldn't blame him.

Leo took another audible breath and after a long pause, the transformation commenced. Betrys stared in a combination of fascination and horror. Surely that must hurt? Or maybe they became used to the way their skin and muscles warped and the snapping and popping as their bones and skin realigned to their alternative form. The shift took precious minutes. They'd be vulnerable at this stage.

Finally, Leo's naked form slumped on the floor in front of them.

Two of his brothers crouched beside him and helped Leo onto the table.

"Betrys," he gasped.

"I'm here." She moved forward.

"Stand on the other side of the table." Saber seemed comfortable bossing them all about. "Give Casey room to work."

"Holy fuck," Sly said. "Look at that sucker."

"It's grown bigger." Betrys stared at the distinct bulge from Leo's stomach. "Much bigger than it was earlier this morn."

"It needs to come out." Saber frowned, and Betrys saw his concern for his younger brother.

Casey examined the instruments and chose a scalpel. "I think it's trying to emerge. Whatever it is, we don't want it running around the room. Make sure the door is locked so no one can enter until we're done. Felix, Saber, I want you to prepare to grab it. Scarlett, you spray the thing with this knock-out solution. I'll tell you when. Wait, everyone put on gloves. We don't want it burrowing into anyone else."

Leo groaned, pain etched into his features. Betrys took his hand and squeezed. This was her fault, and she intended to stand by his side and help correct the consequences of her actions.

"Right." Casey scanned their faces, her manner calm despite the simmering tension that filled the room. "Everyone ready?"

"Do it." Leo's pained groan made the hair at the back of Betrys's neck prickle.

"I'm injecting the area," Casey said in a level voice. Her face was serious, her concentration absolute.

A woman who handles herself well in a crisis, Betrys thought. Good, Leo needed stellar people on his side.

Leo grunted, his big body arching upward as the thing in his stomach protested the numbing agent Casey injected. It bucked and writhed beneath Leo's skin.

Casey picked up the medical wand and made an incision.

Iseult screamed, daggers of pain transmitting from her head to the myriad tiny hooks on the ends of her legs. White-hot and searing, it was agonizing. Too much to bear. She collapsed onto the white floor of her web and curled into a ball. The two on-duty guards rushed to her aid, but she struck out at them. Hissed. One of her feet caught a guard in the leg, jerking him off balance. He toppled with a loud thump then tried to scuttle from her reach.

Iseult screeched, the torture indescribable. The agony came from inside, radiated outward, much like her web.

"Take me to Tiraq," she ordered, the words sharp and clipped in the Spiderus language. "Six guards. Don't care what that manager at the resort says." As soon as she relayed the command, some of the pain inside her subsided—enough for her mind to clear. Tiraq. Yes, gut instinct told her she needed to travel. Every part of her shouted the action was necessary.

"When do you want to leave, my lady?" one of the guards asked.

"Now. No, wait. Tomorrow. We will need to make preparations, gather weapons." The blast of pain tailed off, Iseult uncurled her limbs and struggled to her feet. "I will prepare. Be ready to depart on the morn."

Betrys couldn't see much because Leo's family crowded him, their faces full of tension, their bodies held in still readiness. She kept holding his hand and watching his expression. He watched her in return, and she caught the strain in his features, the worry, a trace of fear, and once again, guilt clawed her mind. All her fault. *All her fault.*

"Not your fault," Leo whispered, his voice harsh.

"Fuck." Saber's voice held shock. "Is that what I think it is?"

"What is it?" Leo growled, a sharp demand. "A worm of some sort?"

"Not exactly," Scarlett said. "It's more of an egg sac."

"Let me lift it out to see what we're dealing with." Casey set down her scalpel and exchanged it for a more suitable instrument.

Leo bit his bottom lip, his fingers clenching hers so tightly Betrys winced at the pressure.

"You're hurting him," Betrys croaked, and Leo slackened his grip a fraction.

"Don't care. *Don't care*. Get it out of me." Leo clenched his jaw.

"I'll do it as fast as I can," Casey said.

Leo moaned and squeezed her hand again. Betrys bit on her tongue, determined not to distract Leo or Casey. They were right. The thing—egg sac or whatever it was—had to come out because it was endangering Leo's health.

"Got it," Casey said in triumph. "Slide that jar over here."

"What is it?" Leo demanded. "What's inside the egg sac?"

"Two creatures. They're insects of some description," Casey replied. "Ugh, they're moving. Quick, put the lid on."

Saber slapped a gloved hand over the top and held up the jar. "Where did you put the vinegar?"

"It's here," Sly said. "I'll pour it into the jar."

"Lid." Saber fastened the top of the large jar then held it to the light.

"Tell me what they are," Leo demanded in a hoarse voice. "I need to know."

"They look like spiders." Betrys pressed a hand to Leo's chest to keep him flat. "Don't move. Casey needs to suture you up."

"Make sure there aren't any more in there," Leo ordered.

"That's what I'm doing," Casey said. "Hand me the sterilizer liquid."

Scarlett passed her the bottle, and Casey sprayed the region.

"No, I don't think anything else is in there. I'm going to close the wound now. We'll know in a couple of days if there are more problems. I couldn't see another foreign object, but we're working blind here. There, all done. You'll know when you're ready to shift."

"As soon as the numbness wears off." Leo glanced at the jar and shuddered. "Are you sure you got them all?"

"I think so," Casey answered.

"Thanks," Leo said in a gruff voice and looked at Saber. "Help me to my room? I'm so tired. Didn't get much sleep last night."

"Sure."

Scarlett held up the jar and studied the contents with a moue of disgust. "They've stopped moving."

"Yeah, I think the vinegar has done the job," Sly said.

Casey set down her needle and stripped off her gloves. "Or it might have been because they weren't quite ready to hatch yet."

"Do you have anything to add, Betrys?" Saber asked.

Betrys shivered in ghoulish fascination as she stared at the things Casey had dug from Leo. "This has never happened before. I don't think Iseult has any idea—that's if she's responsible."

"She must be," Felix said. "It's too much of a coincidence that they grew in the wound she inflicted."

Betrys nodded. "Iseult's behavior has been off recently. Her guards too. I thought...maybe... I don't know what I thought. I've never seen them act with...with such exuberance." She shivered. "They've been singing, and it's plain creepy."

"While Leo is sleeping, we'll work out a plan to retrieve your son." Saber helped Leo off the table.

"In my room," Leo said. "Need Betrys to stay with me."

Saber frowned, his forehead furrowing, before he gave a clipped nod. Shades of Leo, Betrys thought. That was what he looked like when he was unhappy or thinking. The brothers were so alike. Even Scarlett's facial expressions fell into line with her brothers. It was very obvious they were siblings.

"I'm in." Felix straightened.

"Me too." Casey's chin lifted in challenge when her husband's face screwed up into what Betrys was beginning to think of as the Mitchell scowl. "I'd be an asset at a clandestine job. You know it."

Felix's frown softened. "I know, sweetheart."

"I'm in," Sly said. "Joe will want to help too."

Saber nodded. "Four of you should be able to do the job."

"She hasn't confirmed her booking yet," Scarlett said. "What if I contacted her and asked if she still wanted to stay at the resort, tell her it's a courtesy call because there is a waiting list of women wanting to holiday at Middlemarch Resort. If she doesn't want to confirm her booking, then we'll give her place to someone else."

Saber helped Leo stand and slipped his arm around Leo's waist. "Good idea. Go do that now, because if Iseult doesn't come to the resort, it will make Ricci's retrieval more difficult."

Ten minutes later, she and Saber were inside Leo's room in his private bungalow.

"Do you think you can shift now?" Saber asked.

"No. Put the jar over there. I want to look at the egg sac later and know the things inside are dead."

Concern flashed across Saber's features as he placed the jar on a shelf filled with entertainment vids. "I'll leave them here. If any of our men are tempted to sign Iseult's contract, we'll show them these."

"Tell them her bite will rot their cock," Leo said. "That should dissuade them." He directed his steps toward his sleep-bed and staggered.

Betrys jumped to his aid, but Saber pounced first and hauled Leo upright. "Let me help you to bed."

"Betrys." Leo's tone reminded her of Ricci when he was

overtired.

"I'm right behind you." She darted around them and hurried to his sleep-bed to draw back the covers.

"I need a coffee," Saber said, once they had Leo tucked up in comfort. "You want one?"

"Yes, please." Betrys paused in the doorway of Leo's bedroom. "I've come to enjoy the Earth beverage."

"Savor it while you can. The replicated stuff tastes of mud, and our stocks are low until we can figure out how to get a new supply or can start growing our own coffee."

"Leo, do you want anything?" Betrys asked from the doorway to the lounge and kitchen area of the bungalow.

"Water, please. A pain pill."

"I'll bring them in. You rest." She entered the food preparing area and found Saber making the coffee. Her steps faltered.

"What?" he asked without a glance over her shoulder.

A raft of goose bumps formed on her skin. Freaky. How had he known she was behind him? She hadn't made a sound.

"Leo wants something for the pain."

Saber turned then, his brow creased in that trademark scowl. "He should be able to shift. That should be his first instinct for self-preservation. He shouldn't be asking for a damn pain pill."

Betrys found herself taking a step backward, her gaze remaining on his agitated face. "D-don't h-hurt me."

Saber straightened, insult replacing his agitation. "I'm not going to hurt you. This isn't your fault."

"But it is. If I hadn't—"

"You were doing what you had to do to protect yourself, your son. Don't apologize for using your survival instincts," Saber said in a hard voice. "I'd do anything to keep my family safe." His mouth quirked giving the Mitchell scowl a new level of brutal intensity. "I have done things I regret in order to help my siblings. Since I've committed the crime, it would be petty of me to resent you for doing the same." He advanced another step, and although instinct told her to run, she forced herself to remain rooted to the spot.

"I-I-"

"I repeat. I am *not* going to hurt you."

A *thump* came from behind her and she whirled around, a tinny *eep* of shock squeezing from her throat. "Leo!" She was at his side in an instant. "Why aren't you resting?"

"Not your fault. Wanted to help my family. Same thing." Beads of sweat covered his forehead. "Not your fault."

"That's what I've been trying to tell her," Saber said. "Betrys, get the pain pills. I saw a bottle on the counter."

On trembling legs, she walked to the kitchen area and poured a glass of water then plucked up the tablets. When she entered the bedroom, Saber had Leo back on the sleep-bed. Leo's face was pale, and he slumped against the headboard, lines of pain etched into his face.

"We'll be in the other room," Saber said once Leo had taken the pills and was reclining on the sleep-bed. "Shout if you want us."

"Betrys," Leo whispered.

She neared the sleep-bed and gazed down at him. "I'm here."

"Don't go," Leo said. "Don't leave me."

"I promise. I'm not going anywhere. Please, Leo. You need to rest, so you can start healing." She waited until his breathing slowed.

"Is he asleep?" Saber asked when she joined him in the other room.

"Yes, I think so. What do you need me to tell you?"

"Start from the beginning." Saber waved her toward a seat. He remained as he was, leaning his backside against the kitchen counter. "From the moment you first met Iseult, and how you came to work for her. I need to know everything you know and have observed about Iseult and her people since your arrival.

Her strengths. Her weaknesses. The weapons she uses to subdue her enemies. Everything." Saber's face was hard and radiated determination.

A shudder crawled Betrys's spine. This man was dangerous, and she didn't want to get on his bad side while he attempted to protect his family.

"Here, drink this." Saber handed her a mug. Tendrils of steam rose from the liquid along with the scent of the coffee beverage.

Betrys wrapped her hands around the mug and took a sip. The bitter black liquid burned her tongue, and she spat it back into the mug.

"Careful, it's hot," Saber said, and a grin flashed across his face. The Mitchell grin she'd witnessed from Leo and from the siblings she'd seen on arrival at the resort. It was obviously a family trait along with the scowl.

Betrys ran her tender tongue over her teeth and winced. She took another cautious sip of her coffee, then started talking, prodded by Saber's questions for clarification.

"So, you see," she finished. "I saw her bite one of her guards a few months ago because he didn't follow orders. Mostly, she rules by fear and the might of her guards. I told you I don't know much."

"No, you've been helpful. We know Iseult is able to paralyze with what we assume is a type of venom, but she prefers to secure them with cuffs. That tells us she has limited ability, or she keeps that talent for emergencies. And she applies the paralyzing agent with her mouth. She seldom leaves her web, which tells us she feels more comfortable on her home turf."

"So what are you going to do?"

"If she contacts you, tell her there are several suitable men here. Tell her they're Leo's brothers, but that you need longer because they're proving difficult and won't sign a contract. See what she says, but try to get her to come to the resort. She's already considered it, and with luck, she'll be easy enough to persuade. Getting her here—to our home ground—would be to our advantage."

"I doubt she'll leave the mansion," Betrys said, shaking her head in support of her words. "She attends the occasional social function but never stays long."

"Because she doesn't enjoy the social scene, or is it for some other reason?" Saber mused. "She never socializes with others of her species?"

"Apart from her guards. She's never had any visitors of the same species."

"There must be a reason for that. Scarlett needs to do more research." Saber set down his coffee and straightened from his lean. "I know it's difficult, but we'll have to get Iseult to come here somehow, so we can snatch your son. Trying to get the better of the woman on her home territory doesn't make sense. I'll be back later. Call me if Leo needs anything."

Betrys wandered after Saber, unsure of what to do next.

"Don't forget. Call me if there are any problems." Saber stepped outside and chuckled when a bright-blue bird waddled up to him. He stooped to pet the strange-looking creature before departing.

What was she meant to do now? Betrys scowled at the closed door.

"Betrys."

The sound of her name galvanized her to action, and she rushed into the bedroom. "What is it? What's wrong? Do you need something else for the pain?"

"No. Come and lie beside me."

"But I might hurt you."

"I need you, Betrys."

CHAPTER ELEVEN

"Hello, Ms. Orna. Welcome to Middlemarch Resort. My name is Saber Mitchell, and I hope you'll contact me should you require any assistance."

"Thank you," Iseult said. "The journey was arduous, and I wish to rest before dinner." Hopefully, she'd make it to her room before she lost grip on her form. Already her eyes flickered with the beginnings of the shift, and she was starting to see everything in multiples of six. A pity because she'd like to cultivate this man. He bore a striking resemblance to Pretty. Another time.

"Space travel does affect some people that way," Saber said. "Here you are. This is one of our best rooms."

He opened the door and stood back to allow her to precede him into a stylish bungalow. Tiles kept the room cool, and the shades of colors were to her taste. But really, she didn't care about the luxurious amenities, styled, according to the brochure, in the way of planet Earth. All she wanted was to be left alone before he discovered her other nature.

"Thank you." *Get rid of him before the change starts. Get rid of him now.* "I have a headache. I rest and recuperate now."

"Of course. Should I send a maid with some blockers?"

"No, I have my own medication."

"I'll leave you then." He paused on the threshold and turned back to her.

A fine view. Pretty view. Pity her control wavered too much for chitchat.

"Just so you know, I've arranged accommodation for your guards at the inn in the village. This resort has a strict policy of females only."

"Yes, of course." Her gaze flickered, and six images of Saber wavered in front of her. "Thank you." She waited, and he stepped outside. Seconds later, he was gone, the door closed behind him.

A groan squeezed past her gritted teeth and her Spiderus shape burst free. The fabric of her white dress split with a loud rent as her extra legs fought to form. Iseult fell forward, dropping to her knees, her mouth wide in a soundless scream. Her humanoid knees reshaped to black and delicate. The change roared over her until nothing of her previous shape remained except her face.

She panted, her central valve speeding at the forceful shift. Normally, she felt stronger in her Spiderus form, but right now a strange weakness gripped her, a peculiar sense of loss. She ached, not in the physical sense, but something that was full of loss and yearning. Emptiness. Confusion and unease drummed at her mind, and she scrutinized her room for danger. Cool tile floors. Not white but cream. Acceptable. Low seats grouped to appreciate the view of the jade-green sea and the bright solar light. A bowl of bright-pink fruit, a contrast to the neutral cream furnishings. Nothing appeared out of place.

She was alone.

Water flowed down her smooth cheek and dropped—a red tear—onto her furry arm as the tangle of emotions inside her fizzled over and became too much, too hard, too difficult for her to contain. The second red tear plopped onto the cream floor tile, and she stared at it, her anxiety ratcheting sharply upward. What was wrong with her? Had she succumbed to an illness of some kind?

Her mind drifted to her remaining family—her older sister, who still lived on Spiderus and acted as the handmaiden to the king. It was worth—no, she couldn't approach Alana. Alana still hadn't forgiven her for *promenading* in the garden with her courtier husband. Finding her younger sister mating in spider form with her husband had pushed Alana to act in a decisive manner. Alana had forced Iseult to leave Spiderus, informing her she returned at her peril.

Alana wouldn't accept Iseult's presence, refused to forgive and forget.

No, her sister would laugh in her face if she sought advice.

Iseult scuttled farther into her two-room suite. The bright solar light had her shying against the wall, her retinas retaining a globe of white for long moments before it faded to normalcy.

"Shutters close. Shutters close. *Shutters close.*" Frantic, her voice rose to a squeak in her panic to avoid the light. A moan of relief slipped from her once the shutters whirred across to mute the brightness. She slumped, her head hanging as she sought the energy to rise.

Now that she was here at the resort, she wondered why she'd been so determined to come. No, not quite true. Pretty's essence had made her giddy with happiness, and she craved a repeat of the experience.

But Pretty was dead.

Betrys had said he had brothers, kinfolk, and she had met one already.

Betrys.

Her assistant would know what to do. Iseult recalled Betrys had said the men were reluctant to sign her contract, even for the remuneration involved. A shudder worked through Iseult—one of pleasure. The piquant flavor of Pretty's semen on her lips, the feel of it splashing against her chest, and driving inside her sheath. The instant his essence had seeped into her skin and trickled down her throat. *Delicious*.

She needed to have that shot of extraordinary substance again.

The flavor had coated her tongue, brought a sense of exuberance.

And she would revel in the repeat taste.

By fair means or foul, since her guards stood ready to rush to her aid. The barrier fence wouldn't keep them out, nor would the two men stationed at the resort entrance. Once her guards controlled the place, there would be nothing to stop her from locking up every single male and taking them at her leisure.

"Yes." A hiss of affirmation. Mr. Saber would start her imbibing. Another hiss escaped, this one of recalled ecstasy and expectation.

And in the meantime, she'd order Betrys to attend her, help her regain her equilibrium. Iseult scampered to her discarded bag and pawed through the contents to find her communicator.

"Betrys," she said in a firm voice, and relaxed once the call process began. It rang for long, long moments, and anxiety clawed up her throat. Where was her assistant? Where was she?

"Betrys Torin," her assistant said in an impatient voice.

"Betrys." Some of the tension in her legs and her shoulders seeped away. "It is Iseult. I have arrived at the Middlemarch Resort and wish to have a meeting to discuss your progress."

"Of course. What is your room number, and when do you wish to meet with me?"

Iseult scrutinized her Spiderus torso and scowled. It would be better if she could be certain of holding her other form. "Tomorrow. We can break our fast together," Iseult said and ignored the faint gasp that came from her communicator. "Arrange a delivery of food for nine hours after the day change. You know what I prefer. I am in the select suite. Make sure you are prompt."

Iseult shut off the communication before her assistant could reply, but she was confident Betrys would follow her orders. The woman from Petros was too terrified of damage to her son to risk disobeying an order.

"What's wrong?" Leo demanded.

After answering her com-circle, the flush of healthy color had left Betrys's cheeks, leaving her as white as the bandage covering his wound. Now she clutched her communicator so hard he feared it might break, and she paced back and forth until her rapid strides started to make him dizzy.

She came to an abrupt halt, her eyes wild with fear. "Iseult is at the resort."

"Saber told us she was here," Leo reminded her, puzzled by her reaction.

"It seems more real now that she's demanding I attend a meeting with her." She bit her bottom lip. "Promise me your younger brothers are responsible. They won't mess up this chance to snatch Ricci?"

"Come here, sweetheart."

She hesitated before closing the distance between them, reluctance in every step. "I don't understand why you're being so nice to me, why your brothers are helping to grab Ricci..." Her shoulders hunched inward. "You were hurt because of me."

"Come here," Leo repeated, his voice a sharp whip of demand. "Lie with me again. I want to talk."

"I need to read my cards. That will tell me what to do."

Leo stared at her departing back and gave a snort of self-derision. All his life he'd found it easy to grab a woman's attention. They took one look at him and almost fell over themselves to please him. Betrys never behaved the same as other women from his past.

On hearing the front door open and close, he laughed aloud.

"Must be losing my touch."

The door opened, and Leo cocked his head. Not Betrys returning.

"Saber." Leo's nostrils flared. "Scarlett. I'm awake. Come and entertain me."

"Where's Betrys?" Saber asked.

"Ugh." Scarlett's nose scrunched as she followed Saber into his bedroom. "Do you have to keep those creepy things on your shelf?"

"Yes," Leo said. "They remind me to look before jumping. Saber, Iseult's arrival has put the fear of God into Betrys. She told me she needed to read her cards."

Saber frowned. "I hope she doesn't lose her nerve. It's too late to call things off now."

"I won't fail," Betrys promised from behind them. "My son's life depends on me. I had to get my cards so I can do a reading. The thing is, what will happen once we have Ricci? Iseult isn't stupid, and it's so unusual for her to go off-planet. She's behaving weirdly, and she's determined to have another man. She wants a Mitchell."

Saber's frown dug deeper into his forehead. "She's not getting one. We can't trust her, and it's not safe. We've all seen what she did to Leo. She almost killed him, and somehow, she laid that egg sac in him. That can't happen—"

"I've got some info," Scarlett burst out, excitement radiating in her restlessness.

"That's what we came to tell you," Saber said dryly.

"I managed to locate a maid who used to work on the

planet Spiderus. In exchange for a free holiday, she answered my questions. And get this, she was there before Iseult left. She told me Iseult was shunned by her kin and forced to leave or face execution because she had an affair with her sister's husband. The maid remembered a huge fuss because not only did they have an affair, but her sister caught them having sex in spider form. For some reason, that's a big no-no."

"Not very honorable," Leo agreed. "But why is that so taboo? The sex in spider form, I mean."

"Because that's the form in which they conceive," Scarlett said. "According to the maid, the males of the Spiderus race are not very fertile. Iseult's sister was furious and blamed Iseult for her husband's misstep."

Betrys sidled a little closer and tugged at her robe. "But Iseult doesn't have any offspring."

"No." Scarlett radiated triumph. "The maid informed me it's possible for the male to pass off his sperm and for the female to hold on to the fertilized egg for years. I think that somehow, Leo triggered something in Iseult, and she released her egg."

"Ugh." Leo shuddered. "Thank God you dug it out of me. The thing is dead, right?"

"Very dead." Saber picked up the jar and studied the contents. "It's not moving any longer. The vinegar has killed it."

"I thought Ma was crazy wanting to bring the contents of her pantry and stocking up on bulky stuff." Scarlett shrugged. "I told her it was a waste of space when we could use my food replicator, but she's saved our skins a few times. Vinegar isn't something I'd consider necessary to replicate later. Burgers and fries, yes. Chocolate." She sent Saber a rueful grin. "I believed I'd packed the important things."

"Maybe Iseult senses her young." Betrys tugged her robe again and darted quick glances at each of them. "The tie between mother and child is strong in most races. Why should Iseult be any different? If what Scarlett says is right, then I don't think Iseult knows or understands what is happening. How old was she when she left Spiderus?"

"She was sixteen cycles, not much more than a child," Scarlett said. "She was given an advisor to go with her."

"The advisor died," Betrys added. "That's why she hired me."

"So you're saying Iseult is working on instinct rather than real knowledge." Leo digested Scarlett's research, but it didn't change his poor opinion of Iseult.

"Iseult isn't much older than Scarlett," Saber said.

"That doesn't give her a pass to kill men," Betrys snapped, her hands fisting at her sides. "She's murdered every man I procured for her, apart from Leo. She keeps Ricci locked away and grants me access to see him when it suits her purposes. And look what she did to Leo. Don't you dare feel sorry for her!"

"She's a murderer." Saber met Betrys's fury with a calm and level stare. "She will be punished."

"How?" Betrys demanded. "How will she suffer? We can't give those men back their lives. Dead is dead."

"Steady, sweetheart." Leo's heart ached for her. While she was still alive, she'd suffered as much as the men who'd lost their lives. Every time she'd recruited a new lover for Iseult, she'd lost a little bit more of herself. "Saber is trying to help."

"Sorry," she whispered and kept her gaze on her feet.

"Look at me," Leo said sharply, his heart drumming against his ribs until Betrys lifted her head. Something in him twisted on seeing her expression.

She reminded him of a dog he'd come across while he was playing by the river with his friend Craig. It had cowered, mistrust shining in its eyes, even though hunger drove the creature close to snatch the food Leo held. He and that dog had spent years together and had hours of fun. Right from the start, he'd known he and the dog that he'd named James were meant to be a team. And now he had the same gut feeling about Betrys.

"Betrys, we need to work together if we want to keep everyone, including you and Ricci, safe. We all have our part to play, but it's a team effort. No one blames you. Shit happens and we deal with the mess together. That's the Mitchell way." Leo glanced away from Betrys to find Saber grinning at him and Scarlett gaping, her mouth open in an unattractive gawk.

Saber's grin held a trace of smugness. "You listened to some of my team talks."

"Hard not to absorb some of your ranting." Leo felt his lips quirk up at the corners. While he'd been in a bad place for months, and yeah, maybe some of it was Betrys's fault, he now knew what he wanted, and it wasn't just revenge. It wasn't just payback and the chance to punch Iseult in her arrogant nose.

He wanted Betrys.

"Betrys is right," Saber said. "We've moved ahead, but we haven't decided what we're going to do once we have Ricci. We need a plan because we can't have Iseult preying on our family or employees. Or other unwary men either."

Scarlett shot a glance at the jar and shuddered. "We can warn our employees. We should inform them."

"We don't want to run the risk of Iseult hearing rumors." Leo understood the sentiment, but there was too much at stake here. "Or suspecting a trap."

"But you can't let Iseult snatch one of your employees either. She expects me to get a man to sign her contract. What am I going to do?"

Saber began prowling around the bedroom. Leo knew his older brother found it easier to think while in motion. He came to an abrupt halt and turned to face them. "Reiterate to her that you're having trouble because the employees are well-paid here. And happy in their work."

"But what if she approaches someone?" Leo asked.

Betrys shook her head. "She won't. At least she hasn't before. I'll know more once I meet her tomorrow morning, but she doesn't recruit the men she feeds off."

"She didn't want to see you earlier?" Scarlett inquired. "Wouldn't she want to castigate you in your failure in finding new prey?"

Betrys sat on the corner of Leo's bed, her robe a swish of white around her slender frame. She pulled a small box from a pocket and turned it around and around in her hands. "Normally, she would, but I told you she's been strange. Unpredictable."

Scarlett chuckled, her amusement billowing out like a fountain. "Tell our employees Iseult has the clap—an alien disease transmitted during sex that will make their willies drop off. Tell them Leo has caught the disease, and authorities have asked us to make sure Iseult isn't able to pass on the disease while they work on extradition orders. Tell them they mustn't discuss the matter with any of the guests."

"Hey!" His sister's impish wink made Leo want to laugh.

"That's too complicated." Saber rejected the idea. "I'll call a meeting with the staff and tell them Iseult refused to have the standard shots to prevent disease and conception, and as such, she may enjoy the facilities but will not be given the freedom to have sex with our employees. I'll tell everyone it's a matter of safety."

"They'll gossip," Scarlett warned.

"I'll tell them anyone who is caught discussing the matter will be sacked." Saber's voice hardened. "They'll believe me."

Betrys hummed at the back of her throat before raising her head. "What about if I tell Iseult I have a selection of possibilities?" she asked, appearing to think aloud. "I could tell her I'd arrange a meeting with each male for her to choose the one she prefers best, then I'll do the negotiations to secure a contract."

"What if she decides to jump the man she's interviewing?" Scarlett asked.

"I don't think she will. She might kill the men she feeds off, but she never touches them or even sees them before I have a signed contract in hand. I had to sign a contract with her too. She is big on getting the terms and remuneration signed off in writing before she acts."

"That might work, and it would allow us all to meet her too. Leo, you can go along in your feline form." Saber's words held an edge of challenge.

"I'll do it." Somehow he'd pull himself together and shift to feline form. "But then what? We can't turn her in to the authorities on Dalcon because that would implicate Betrys. And what's to stop her from grabbing any one of us and not bothering about her precious contract?"

"All I can tell you is that she has never done that before. She insists on a signed contract first. I don't know why, and I haven't pushed because of her threats regarding Ricci." She turned the box in her hands before looking up and scanning faces. "What if we reported her to her own people? Would they do something to stop rumors from spreading about their race? In fact, there's nothing to stop us contacting them now and putting things in motion."

"I can do that," Scarlett agreed. "I'll contact the maid and find out who we should approach."

"Done." Saber headed for the door. "I'll call a meeting. Get some rest, Leo. I'll get the kitchen to send you a meal."

"Thanks," Leo said.

Everyone filed out of his room until only he and Betrys remained.

"I hope this works." Leo cautiously shifted to find a more comfortable spot and to release some of the tension left behind.

"If contacting the Spiderus people doesn't work, I'll report Iseult to the authorities on Dalcon myself. She can't be allowed to feed on and kill men any longer."

"Or we could just kill her." Leo indicated her box of cards with a jerk of his head. "Let's see what your cards say."

Betrys woke early, before the light of the solar star pierced the darkness of the night. For a time, she attempted to drop back to the state of slumber, but her mind ran a busy path and refused to settle.

"If you can't sleep, we can do other things," Leo said.

"What sort— No! You're still recovering from your wound. Lights on. Low illumination."

"No problem. I'll let you do all the work." Leo kicked off the covers to reveal his nakedness. His cock thrust upward, and he wore a distinct smirk. "It's too soon to contact the twins about your son."

Betrys tried to ignore his cheekiness, tried to tell herself she needed to get out of bed and prepare for the coming meeting with Iseult. She tried and failed, seduced by the twinkle in his eyes. Scooting closer, she placed her hand on his hip, below the white dressing on his stomach, and used her fingertips to trace his silky skin.

Fire and chills warred within her body, and her mind leaped onto the same page as Leo's. She moved her fingertips lower, one finger stroking down the crease of his thigh and torso.

"Is that all you're going to do?"

"No."

"Well?"

"I know you're bossy. Are you going to order me around now too?"

"I could tell you what to do, tell you how I prefer to be touched."

Betrys bit back a smile. "Thank you for the kind offer, but I think I can handle this on my own. I'd like some information first.

How are you feeling?"

"Fit enough to fuck," Leo said.

Betrys wanted to smile again. "Well, in that case." She gripped his shaft and encased the tip with her mouth, taking him deep and sucking hard.

He gave a startled grunt then groaned, his hips lifting as she retreated, her mouth rising to his tip. Betrys laughed around his cock, loving the power and the way she could draw a response from him without trying hard. She sucked him deep again and used her tongue to explore the head and taste him. With her hand, she palmed one of his balls while she ran her tongue over the swollen head of his cock.

"Betrys." Desire and wonder filled his taut voice. "Aw, fuck. Betrys."

She varied her touches, giving him the lazy stroke of her tongue followed by more suction. Her hands explored the base of his shaft and his upper thighs.

A rush of moisture gathered in her pussy, an intense burst of heat making her want to squeeze her legs together. Goddess, she'd wanted to tease Leo, but it seemed she was succeeding in turning herself on too.

She raked her tongue over the head of his cock and was gentler on the underside. A dark sound—almost pleading—issued from his throat. Her name was a garbled groan from his lips.

Another laugh spilled from her, vibrating around his cock. He shuddered, his hands holding her head in place and tugging her hair from her braid. She set up a quick rhythm. Lick and suck. Lick and suck.

Leo started to tremble, and his hips canted upward. The scent of him filled her nostrils, and his flavor filled her mouth. His fingers laced in her hair, his cock swelling within her mouth. She cleaned away the fluid gathering at his slit, and he gave a raw and guttural groan. She sucked hard once more and his cock jerked, semen shooting down her throat as he climaxed. She swallowed automatically, drinking him down until the pulses slowed and ceased.

"Thank you," Leo said as she released him and lifted her head. "Now it's my turn. Lose your clothes, scoot up the bed, and straddle my head."

Betrys frowned before moving. The curl of arousal spiraling low in her abdomen overrode her reluctance to obey his request. Without breaking his gaze, she slipped off the bed and unfastened the thin gown she wore beneath her robe. It glided to the floor with a swish. She stepped from the circle of fabric and returned to the bed, positioning herself above his head.

She swallowed, feeling strange and a little vulnerable.

Leo's grin was quick and bright and desire stirred, hot and expectant in her quim. His fingers curled around her thighs, his eyes heavy-lidded as he stared up at her. The first lazy stroke of his tongue dragged a gasp from deep in her chest.

"Like that, huh?" Her juices made his lips shine. "You taste good, sweetheart."

She stared at him, part of her still unable to believe she was here with Leo, in his bed, engaging in sex.

Good sex.

Hot sex.

Amazing sex.

He licked again and applied the gentle suction of his mouth. A noise escaped her, low and breathy and hungry.

"Leo, I need...I want... Oh-oh, yes. Goddess. Just there. Right there."

Leo tongued her. Goddess, he knew what to do with every part of his body. She writhed above him, rapidly losing her reservations about the position.

"Leo, I—" She broke off when he hit a sensitive spot. Sparks of electricity sizzled and ignited in her, and a moan rolled up her throat and out. "Goddess."

He flailed her clit with his tongue again and hit a sweet spot. She exploded into her orgasm, her thighs quaking as she attempted to remain in place.

Long seconds later, Leo lifted her up with easy strength, and she flopped over on her side, her muscles still humming with residual satisfaction. He drew her against his chest and kissed her straight on the lips.

He tasted of her.

"It's still early. Let's get some more sleep."

Heavy-eyed, she yawned and cuddled beside him, taking care not to put pressure on his stomach wound. She sighed and yawned again. He smelled so good and for the first time in many cycles, she felt secure. Safe.

"Betrys. Betrys, sweetheart."

Someone grasped her arm and shook.

"Wake up. We've slept too long. You need to go to meet Iseult."

"Goddess." Betrys jerked from her drowsiness and leaped off the sleep-bed.

"Fuck," Leo said.

She glanced over her shoulder and winced on seeing Leo with his hand pressed against his wound. "My apologies."

"It's...okay," Leo replied through gritted teeth. "I'm all right."

Betrys scrambled into her clothes and twitched the fabric of her robe into place. "I'm late. Iseult will be furious. Where are my shoes? Have you seen them?"

"Under the low table in the lounging room."

Betrys hurried out to the other room, spied her shoes, and thrust her feet into them. "I'll see you later."

"Betrys."

Leo limped from the room and halted in front of her. He tucked a lock of brown hair behind her ear. "Be careful. You have your com-circle?"

"Yes." She slipped her right hand into her pocket to double-check for the rigid communicator. Along with her com, she felt the sheath of the knife that Caspar had gifted her.

"Felix is going in with you."

"No. We should save that for another occasion." She placed her fingers over his lips to halt his objections. "I promise I'll be fine. Iseult has never physically harmed me. Her threats are always directed at Ricci. When do you think we'll hear from your brothers?"

"Soon," Leo promised. "We'll hear something while you're dealing with Iseult." Leo bent and kissed her slow, tender, and when he lifted his head, she drew in a sharp breath. The man kissed with skill. "Be safe, sweetheart."

"Always." She forced a smile to hide the nerves dancing in the pit of her stomach. Failure wasn't an option.

Betrys had to force herself to follow the gravel path that wound through the plants and fragrant blooms. A selection of variegated blue leafy bushes lined the path, their vivid blue and white flowers perfuming the air with the same spice scent of the cookie things Eva and Anna produced in the resort kitchens. They gave way to tall trees with bright coral trunks. Their green and coral foliage cast shade over the gravel walkways. Despite the sweet scent and the beautiful surroundings, the distant music from the waves coming to shore, her gut churned with apprehension. She had to manage Iseult and make sure her suspicions weren't aroused.

Betrys exited the trees and caught glimpses of the jade-green sea. The waves were louder now and tumbled to shore, several guests already swimming and enjoying walks along the shore.

Betrys lifted her chin and approached the large bungalow. She knocked on the door, a sound behind her attracting her attention.

"Perfect timing," she said to the droid waitress who wheeled a trolley of food toward the bungalow. "Let me take that for you."

Betrys knocked on the door again, and on hearing a summons

to enter, she wheeled the trolley into Iseult's room.

Iseult sat in a chair, the light muted by the drawn shutters. The woman seemed to have shrunk in the short time since Betrys had seen her last.

Betrys hid her frown. "Would you like me to serve your meal first, before I make my report?"

Iseult gave a curt nod, then appeared to drift with her own thoughts because she barely blinked when Betrys dropped one of the covers the kitchen had placed over the meal. She placed the food in front of Iseult, poured her a glass of cool water and took a cup of coffee for herself. The stuff was addictive and seemed to wake her up.

"What is that scent?" Iseult asked in an abrupt voice. "It seems familiar."

"It's the coffee."

Iseult picked up her glass and took a sip. Her hand trembled, and Betrys concealed her astonished reaction.

"You were late."

"I needed to collect the breakfast." It was surprising how easy it was to lie, how the false words rolled off her tongue when so much was at stake.

"False," Iseult said. "I heard the vibrations of a second being."

Betrys felt herself blink.

"Why were you late?" Iseult leaned closer, her nostrils flaring.

"I slept in."

"Truth." Iseult drank more water without taking her penetrating gaze off Betrys.

Don't move. Don't blink. Don't let Iseult suspect there is a plot afoot.

Iseult leaned forward, sniffed the air around Betrys. "You don't smell right." Her nostrils quivered. "The scent on your skin is combined with another. Have you been with a man?"

Heat burst in Betrys's face and a croaking sound emerged from her throat. "I-I—"

Iseult leaned back, more her old self—unpredictable and in charge. "Don't bother to deny it. What I want to know is why you're enjoying yourself, partaking of the resort amenities, when I sent you here to do a job." Her gaze journeyed up and down Betrys until it landed back on Betrys's face, and she scowled. "Why would a man spend time with you when he could have me and get paid for the episode? Is this man blind?"

A lump bloomed in Betrys's throat, blocking her emotions and the mechanism of successful speech. She bit her bottom lip and concentrated on keeping a professional image.

"I need a man," Iseult said.

Betrys wanted to tell Iseult that most women wooed on their own. She wanted to tell Iseult that Leo appeared to enjoy taking her to bed. She wanted to tell Iseult to get fucked, and not in the way she wanted.

But she knew better.

Control was the key here. Hidden by the folds of her robe, she balled her hands into tight fists, dug her fingernails into her palms. *Control.*

Instead of replying, Betrys said the words that tingled on her lips in her mind. *Get fucked, Iseult.*

The act of rebellion cheered her, lent steel to her backbone, and she lifted her chin. "I have a suggestion. I could arrange for several suitable men to come and meet you, and you can put your case to them yourself. Maybe if they met you in person, your offer of employment would prove more attractive."

A slow smile curled across Iseult's lips, and Betrys knew the woman liked the idea. She thought she'd sweet talk every man she met into signing her contract. Betrys knew that wouldn't happen.

"Should I arrange the meetings?"

"Yes. That is a good idea. Arrange this for tomorrow. That will give me time to recover from the journey and refresh."

"Of course," Betrys said. "Was there anything else you required before I leave?"

"No, you may go. Report back to me tonight before dinner."

"Should I order dinner for you?"

"Yes, make sure you order fruit nectar and red meat. I wish to build my strength."

"Of course." Betrys turned away to unload the various plates of food items before wheeling the trolley to the door.

"Oh, Betrys."

Betrys turned to face her employer. "Yes?"

"I expect you to work, not play with the resort employees. You are here to do a job, and your son's safety depends on your success in recruiting a man for my use."

CHAPTER TWELVE

Leo paced his rooms while waiting for Betrys to return from her interview with Iseult. The woman was evil, and despite Betrys's assumption that Iseult wouldn't attack her, there was always a first time.

A tap sounded on the door, and long strides took him there. He wrenched the door open.

"It's you," he said to his oldest brother and glanced along the gravel path. He couldn't see Betrys. "I thought it would be Betrys."

"She still with Iseult?"

"Yeah."

Saber pushed Leo back and stepped inside. "I've heard from Sly and Joe. They think it will be easy enough to snatch Ricci and intend to go in tonight. Sly said they'll ring us as soon as they have Betrys's son."

"Good."

"How are you feeling? You're moving better—not so hunched over."

"I'm fairly sure I'll be able to shift."

"Do it," Saber said. "You'll heal quicker."

"Not until I speak with Betrys."

"Are you playing her?"

"What? No!" His denial was an explosion of sound. "It started out that way. You know it did. But once I learned about her son—hell—before that I started to like her. She's done the best she could to keep her and her son alive. I thought about her situation, and once I decided I would've done the same thing, some of my anger faded."

"Some?"

"If I come face-to-face with Iseult, I'll be tempted to attack first and ask questions later."

The door opened and Betrys glided into the room.

"How did it go?" Saber asked.

"She thought it was a good idea and wants me to arrange the meeting for tomorrow. She doesn't look well."

"Don't feel sorry for her," Leo snapped.

"I don't. She told me I was here to work, not sleep with the merchandise. Then she implied I was ugly and the man who slept with me needed glasses."

"Bitch," Leo said.

"I'm not beautiful." Betrys sounded neutral.

Damn. She was thinking too hard and coming up with the wrong answers. If only they'd had more privacy. He sighed. "Saber heard from the twins. They've reconnoitered and intend to snatch your son tonight. They'll contact us as soon as they have him safe."

Betrys nodded, and when he went to her and wrapped his arm around her waist, she stiffened and moved away.

"I'll arrange five men to see Iseult and explain the circumstances," Saber said. "Scarlett hasn't heard back from her contact yet, so we wait."

"I don't need to report back to Iseult until dinner hour tonight. Can I have a list by then?"

"I'll have it ready for you this afternoon. Leo, why don't you take Betrys to our private beach? I'll ask the kitchen to prepare a picnic basket for you."

Relief shot through Leo. Time alone was what they needed. "Make sure we're not interrupted unless it's an emergency."

Saber grinned, and Leo realized his big brother was doing a lot of that lately. Mating with Eva had brought happiness to his brother's life, and it was rubbing off on all of them. The opportunities their people had now, due to the new businesses Eva and Casey had started, made everyone happier and more settled. They'd even started trading with the Froggish people who lived deep in the jungle, a few days' trek inland.

"I should stay at the resort and speak with the staff," Betrys said.

A stubborn woman and a silly one, if she thought he intended to walk away. He was capable of deciding on the woman he'd like as a mate, and physical appearance meant nothing to him. People had judged him all his life on his looks instead of trying to see the man beneath the good genes. He, better than anyone, knew appearances didn't mean a damn. Pretty and attractive faces didn't make the person good. Often, it made them selfish and self-centered, and they were qualities he refused to have in his mate.

"No, I want to—need to get out of these rooms before I go crazy. Someone should stay with me in case I have a problem."

Saber came to his rescue by adding his support. "Would you go with Leo, please, Betrys? I need to speak with my employees and monitor Iseult. From what we've learned, I think she'll stay holed up in her room, but I intend to place a couple of guards on her bungalow. I need to organize that too. If we hear anything further from Sly and Joe, I'll contact you. Take your com-circle with you."

"All right," Betrys said after a long pause. "I'll babysit Leo."

Leo bit his tongue, but his big brother laughed under his breath. Betrys never registered, but Leo's feline senses heard just fine. He shot a warning at Saber and received a wink in return.

"I'll meet you here late afternoon," Saber said.

"Can you give me brief details of their physical appearance too? Iseult will ask. She's rather particular in that way."

"What type of man does she prefer?"

Betrys glanced from Leo to Saber and back. "Tall and fit build and a pleasing appearance. Any man who looks like both of you."

Saber grinned. "Done deal."

"Do you want to have a shower?" Leo asked once his brother had left.

"Not you too," Betrys muttered and stomped off. Seconds later, Leo heard the sanitizer start.

"I'll take that as a yes." Leo thought for a second and picked up his communicator to ring Casey, his sister-in-law, and the manager of the resort boutique. There was nothing wrong with Betrys's figure. Maybe if she started dressing in something other than her robe, she might start to feel better about herself.

With his call made, he stalked to the small en suite sanitizer room. The wound in his stomach was healing well, and once they arrived at the beach, he'd try shifting.

He peeled off his clothes and stepped into the cleansing unit.

"What are you doing?" She glared at him through wet hanks of hair. "Can't a woman have some privacy?"

"I thought we'd save time," Leo said. "Let me help you wash your hair." He picked up a soap tab and lathered it between his palms.

Her scowl changed, shifting to wary. Maybe a trifle confused, he decided. Good, because she was kicking him off-balance too.

He lathered the cleanser, patiently massaging her skull. Warm water poured over them, the faint metallic scent indicating it came from their recycle plant. Gradually, she relaxed, her shoulders settling into a more normal posture.

He rinsed her hair, then briskly washed his own body. "My mother makes a conditioner for the ladies to rub into their hair. It smells of coconuts, and my sister says it works well."

"What's a coconut?"

"It's a plant that grows on Earth. I don't know how my mother replicated the scent, but she's good at stuff like that. Finished? Good. Let's dry off and hit the beach."

Somehow, Betrys found herself organized and sitting on a private beach. She wore a black, white and red wrap with what Leo told her were turtle designs. Another Earth thing, according to Leo.

They sat under a shady thatched umbrella. Leo was stretched out on his wrap, his body naked and relaxed, his eyes closed. His breathing was even, and she thought he was asleep. Her mind too full of worry about Ricci to rest, she fidgeted in her effort to find a comfortable spot. That done, her gaze wandered Leo's chest and came to a screeching halt at his stomach. Her mouth fell open. Magic. It was magic. The flesh had knitted together overnight, although the scar appeared scarlet against his tanned skin. She hadn't noticed earlier in the shower.

"Stop staring."

"You look at me. I was returning the compliment." Despite her anxiety, her longing to hug her son in person to assure herself of his safety, she couldn't help but smile at Leo. Even with his scars, he was a beautiful specimen. At the thought, some of her feel-good mood packed a bag and sneaked off for a happier hangout. When she picked the scabs off the known facts and her involvement, she came up with the only possible answer.

"Why are you paying attention to me?" She winced at her runaway tongue, then decided to continue because the subject was worrying her. "I don't understand why we're here at the beach. I'm sure you have better things to do."

A frown creased Leo's brow, and his eyes snapped open. He propped himself up on one arm, his look intense and thoughtful. He stared at her without saying anything, the silence stretching out until it became uncomfortable. "Whatever you're thinking, you're wrong. If I didn't want to spend time with you, I wouldn't. It's as simple as that."

"But Iseult—"

"At this moment I don't give a flying fuck about Iseult," Leo snapped. "Once we get Ricci back and this business with Iseult is over, what would you like to do?"

Betrys frowned. "I'll have to find a new job. Hopefully, I can retrieve my stash of money from the mansion." Her shoulders slumped because the chances of that weren't good.

"That's easy," Leo said. "We'll contact the twins and tell them where you've hidden your currency. They can collect it at the same time they retrieve Ricci."

Hope sprang to life in her, and her gaze snapped to his face. "Really?"

"Sure. We'll contact them now." Leo reached for his com. "Sly," he said, and just like that, he spoke with his younger brother and handed over his communicator for her to relay the details.

"Thank you," she whispered, her heart full of hope. "That money will mean I can find decent lodgings in Dalcon city and give me breathing space if I'm not able to secure a job straight away."

"Why do you want to go back to Dalcon? You could stay here. There are other kids in the village, and Ma was muttering about starting a school the other day. We need help at reception. I know that because we're keeping Scarlett busy with other stuff."

"No, I think it might be better if I leave. My presence will remind everyone of the bad things—"

"Bull crap," Leo snapped. "Has it occurred to you that I want you to stay?"

She stared at him, shocked to the core by his words and the

underlying anger in them.

He laughed without warning, and that made her frown harder.

"I might try to shift and then have a swim," he said, changing the subject. "Will you swim with me?"

"I can't swim in this." She indicated her wrap.

"Take it off. No one comes to this beach apart from my family. They know we're here and they won't interrupt us unless it's an emergency." He stood and extended his hand.

She took it, and he hauled her to her feet. Deft fingers untwisted the knot at her breasts and before she could gather a protest, the silky fabric fluttered to the sand, leaving her naked.

"I'm going to shift now," Leo said. "Fingers crossed that everything goes as it should."

Betrys stood back and watched Leo. The transformation from humanoid to feline seemed to take even longer than the first time she'd seen him shift. The sounds of bones cracking and reshaping made her wince. Then, Leo stood before her in leopard form, his sides heaving with exertion and his maw open wide while he panted.

"Do you want some water?"

He grunted once. Once for yes, she recalled, and reached for the water bottle. She was unsure of what to pour the water into then noticed the shallow bowl in the basket of food someone had packed for them. She poured water for Leo and waited while he drank his fill.

The solar star was hot on her bare skin, and when Leo ambled into the jade water, she followed him.

"It's cold," she shrieked.

Leo grunted and he gamboled around her, splashing her with more cool water, his mouth open in a kind of a feline smirk. The expression on his face, the humor in his familiar green eyes reminded her of her son. For once it was a good memory, one of fun and games, and she laughed out loud and scooped up water in her hands to splash him in the face.

He let out a strange, yet heart-warming bark of laughter and burst into a frenzy of movement, splashing them both.

"Right," she said. "This is war."

They played and giggled and splashed each other until they were both soaked and Betrys warded him off with raised hands.

"Enough," she said, still chuckling.

Leo exited the sea and shook himself with vigor.

"Hey!"

Leo flicked his tail and trotted up the beach to where their belongings lay on the sand. Betrys paused to release her hair from its scraggly bun and wrung out the excess water.

"Hurry up, slowpoke," Leo called.

Betrys glanced in the direction of his shout. "You shifted." She hurried across the sand. "Are you all right? How do you feel? Do you need to take more painkillers?"

"I'm fine." Leo cupped her face and smiled. "Saber was right. I feel much better after my shift, and the transformation was much easier just now. I'm starving. Do you want something to eat?"

He grabbed her hand and tugged her onto the blanket they'd spread out earlier. His gaze wandered her bare shoulders and followed the progress of a droplet of water as it dripped off a tendril of hair and rain over her collarbone and down, down across the curve of her breast.

"Or maybe we'll eat later." He leaned closer to lick the bead of water off her skin.

Her breath caught and caught again when his mouth shifted to settle on one nipple. Instead of sucking, he delicately licked, his tongue a brand on her senses.

Betrys clutched his shoulders and clung, her head tipping back as she thrust her breasts forward in a silent demand for more. "Leo." She followed up with a verbal entreaty. "Please."

He lifted his head, his eyes doing a weird shift to partial feline.

"I do please." And he pushed her back onto the blanket and rose over her. "I want you. I always want you."

"You do?" She bit her lip on hearing the insecurity in her tone, but the truth was Iseult had dented her confidence, made her doubt herself and wonder about Leo's intentions. She tried not to dwell on things outside her control. Yes, once Ricci was safe she could move on and create a new, safe future for both of them.

"One day you won't doubt me." Leo's voice took on a hard edge. "I understand more than you think, which is why I'm willing to give you a chance to accept this, us."

"We're friends."

He gave a sharp shake of his head, his eyes shifting even more catlike. "We're more."

"But—"

"Enough," Leo barked, and he kissed her in a possessive manner as if to make sure she didn't speak at all.

Betrys surrendered and held him close, kissing Leo back with the same urgency. His hands started to wander, exploring the parts of her he could reach. One breast. Her hip. He kissed her until raw need chased them both, and her lips were swollen and tender. His mouth traveled across her cheek, then followed her neck, taking tiny bites that made her nerve endings salute with excitement. Tendrils of desire crawled over her skin, slid through her veins to settle between her legs.

"Leo, please. I want you inside me, filling me."

"You want me to fuck you?" he demanded.

Her eyes flew open, and their gazes met. No. No, that wasn't what she wanted, and she saw he knew it too.

"Or do you want me to make love with you?" he whispered, his breath hot against her ear. His finger circled one of her nipples, the gentle friction driving her to distraction. She shuddered at his repeat of the action and the slow slide of his tongue. "You tell me what you want."

"I want you. Make love to me. Please."

"My pleasure, sweetheart." He parted her legs with a decisive shove of his thigh between hers. She was wet and needy, the air cool on her hot flesh.

Somewhere overhead, a bird called and the solar sun shone down. His masculine scent filled each of her breaths while frissons of excitement danced across every inch of her skin.

When he guided his cock into her warmth, she swallowed and arched her hips to take him deeper. Her mouth was dry, her heart thudding, her quim on fire for his possession.

"Leo, yes," she cried.

He forged into her flesh, stretching and filling her slick channel. "Fuck, you feel good. So perfect." He pulled back and drove in again, and they gave a unified groan.

He feasted on her mouth, then lifted his head to reposition his attentions. He scraped his teeth over the fleshy part where her shoulder and neck met and on his next hard thrust, he bit down.

The unexpected pain brought a spike of pleasure, a surge of wetness, and a rough growl vibrated in his chest. His cock seemed to swell inside her as his tongue licked across the sensitive flesh of her upper shoulder.

She moaned, arched upward to take his hard strokes, the sweet rub of his flesh against her clit. She soared, feeling as if she were flying out of her skin. Leo kissed the spot again, and everything pulled tight inside her, detonating with a suddenness that yanked a scream from deep in her chest. It was hard to breathe, hard to contain the sensations coursing through her, hard to believe she was naked with Leo.

His tongue worked back and forth over the spot where he'd bitten her, and that seemed to prolong the spasms of pleasure. He bit her again, the wet rasp of his tongue sliding across her flesh and chasing away the prick of pain.

He shoved into her, and she clung, letting him take what he

needed. Then he lifted his head and cried out with a harsh groan of enjoyment. She caught his next moan with her mouth and held him as his orgasm thundered through him. His large form shuddered as he dragged out every last sensation then stilled.

"Aw, sweetheart." His mouth curved into a seductive smile, and his fingers smoothed across the spot where he'd bitten her.

She shivered, and her quim gave a sharp pulse around his cock. "Do that again."

His fingers stroked back and forth, a hint of smugness sliding into his expression. "Feel good?"

"Yes."

Leo pressed his forehead against hers, his lips curving upward at the corners. "I think it was fuckin' great." He speared his fingers into her wet tendrils of hair. "I like this loose. Why do you never wear it this way?"

"It gets in the way..." She sighed. "No, that's not the truth. I've noticed how Iseult yanks on hair, and I saw her grab one of the servants by his hair tentacles one day. She yanked two of the tentacles off, and he almost died because I had difficulty halting the loss of life force." Horror filled her at the memory of the streams of purple life force spurting between her fingers and pooling on the floor. "He ran off after that, and luckily for him, Iseult's men didn't find him."

"That's why I shaved off my hair."

Betrys pulled back, then reached for his hands and squeezed them in sympathy. "I'm sorry. So sorry that I dragged you into Iseult's world."

"It's in the past now. Besides, if I'd walked away from the contract offer, we wouldn't be here now."

She didn't have the same facility to forgive and found it difficult to believe Leo and his family could find the generosity to let her error of judgment go. "When do you think we'll hear from your brothers?"

"Later tonight. Don't worry. Sly and Joe will come through. Saber wouldn't have sent them if he didn't think they could do the job. Are you hungry? I am."

"I can't help but worry," Betrys said.

"Don't." Leo rubbed his finger across the spot where he'd bitten her.

It should have hurt, considering his sharp teeth, but each time he touched her there, a spike of sexual heat landing with a sizzling pulsation in her quim. "What are you doing to me?"

"Touching you." Leo's lazy satisfaction came through clearly as his gaze drifted across her face to land on the spot he stroked.

The needy heat coalesced low, but this time her stomach rumbled, and he laughed at her heated cheeks.

"But I'd better feed you because you'll need your strength."

A sense of breathlessness grabbed her, slapped heat to her cheeks while she stared, unable to summon words to reply.

"That's a promise," he said in his husky voice, and he didn't need to touch her to send messages of lust bolting from head to toe. His heated gaze did that on its own.

The scent puzzled Iseult for the entire day. She ate the food Betrys had ordered for her and dined heartily—better than she'd eaten for eons. Her limbs shook less and although her busy mind hadn't let her sleep for long, she felt stronger and eager to seek out her next essence donor.

That thought sent her mind back to her timid assistant. She hadn't behaved as normal. *She's more...confident and assured,* Iseult thought with a frown. Since their last meeting, her assistant had found a backbone.

"Hard to imagine a man wanting to fuck her," Iseult thought

aloud. "But at a resort such as this, a man would offer himself... Or maybe she used one of the fantasy rooms and became aroused. Yes, yes. That could have happened, yet her scent is overlaid with another."

The scent, the memory of it continued to niggle at her.

Iseult poked through her mind and froze when the answer came to her.

Betrys smelled of Pretty.

No. No, that couldn't be right. Pretty had succumbed to her demands and died after she'd sucked him dry of essence.

Iseult sniffed the air and caught faint tendrils of the scent. She halted to puzzle over the information while she drew the fragrance deep into her lungs.

Betrys and Pretty?

No, impossible.

But Pretty did have brothers who lived here, and her assistant was having sex with one of them or coming in close contact, near enough for their body scents to mingle, when she should be working to contract their services for her. Iseult started to pace, angry stomps as her feet struck the tiles. The *tap-tap-tap, tap-tap-tap* of her rapid steps matched the rapid pounding of her heart.

No. No. Betrys hadn't received that scent from a fantasy room, nor had she received it while brushing past one of Pretty's kin. No, this scent was deep within her, had seeped into her pores. Plain Betrys was fucking the man meant for her.

She would stop this.

She would halt this now, and Betrys would pay for her double-crossing, deceit. The effrontery. The audacity of the woman.

Oh yes. Betrys Torin would rue her mistake in trying to cheat Iseult Orna.

CHAPTER THIRTEEN

"Iseult attack. Iseult punish now." Iseult was halfway to the door before she realized she was in Spiderus form. No, a plan. She needed a strategy. Iseult stewed, she cursed, she scuttled around her bungalow for the rest of the day while she pondered her method of attack. Several scenarios occurred, and she rejected each before coming to a final decision.

The perfect way to gain payback for Betrys's betrayal.

Iseult stomped over to her communicator. "Head guard," she demanded. She tapped her two front feet on the tiles in an impatient *rat-a-tat-tat. Rat-a-tat-tat. Rat-a-tat-tat.*

"Yes, mistress," the man replied in a prompt and obliging manner.

"I require your services later tonight. Please come to the resort and wait outside the fence until I call. The barrier surrounds the resort, but a Spiderus will have no trouble jumping."

"Yes, mistress. We come now."

"I will call you with details," Iseult said and cut the call.

Now she would practice her shifting. For her plan to work, she must walk through the resort in her humanoid form. Yes, more food for strength. That would make a good start.

"How much longer?" Betrys asked.

Leo bit back a smartass comment. If he stood in Betrys's shoes, he'd act crazy too. "You know the plan, sweetheart. Joe and Sly are entering the mansion after dark. You gave them the code for the gate, and they reported that there are minimal guards. They will call as soon as they're clear."

"I don't care about the currency. I can earn more," Betrys said. "I just want my son."

"We'll get Ricci. Try not to worry."

A tap sounded on the door, and Leo went to answer, cracking it open a fraction before he opened it.

Saber entered, carrying a tray, and Eva followed him.

"We brought dinner." Eva's bright-blue eyes held curiosity as her gaze darted to Betrys. "I hope you don't mind, but we decided to eat with you. Tell us if we're spoiling any romantic plans." A saucy wink winged in Saber's direction, then she ducked her head and allowed a lock of smooth blonde hair to screen her expression.

His older brother grinned, and once the trays were on the table in the dining area, he wrapped his arm around his slim wife and dragged her against his side. "Too bad if they object. They've had all day with just the two of them."

"Betrys could do with the distraction." Leo shot a quick look at her. "She's worried about her son."

"Sly and Joe contacted me a short while ago," Saber said. "That's another reason we decided to invite ourselves for dinner. The remaining staff seem to be having a party in Iseult's absence."

Betrys gaped at Saber. "A party? That's not sanctioned by Iseult. She'll be furious if she discovers this."

"I didn't think so. That's what Eva and I decided during the walk here."

Leo witnessed the exact moment his brother noticed the mating mark on Betrys. In the hours since he'd bitten her, the wound had closed over and, although he hadn't examined the mark, he thought a tiny black cat tattoo was forming—just like the ones Eva and Casey bore.

Betrys wouldn't leave him anytime soon, not since both he and his feline had claimed her as their mate. The knowledge brought a wealth of satisfaction, and he wanted to shout the news to everyone in the resort who would listen. Maybe later. First, they needed to rid themselves of Iseult.

Saber opened his mouth, but Leo gave a faint shake of his head.

"What did Iseult do today?" Leo asked.

"She stayed in her bungalow. No one has seen her, apart from room service. We sent Casey to deliver her meal instead of the new droids Scarlett has designed for the purpose," Saber said. "Casey reported that she answered the door in humanoid form."

Betrys drew a sharp breath. "She must be feeling better. Until Leo— I'd never seen her in her spider form."

A loud squawk outside the door had them all turning in that direction.

"Sorry." Eva pulled a face. "That sounds like Bluebird."

"Let him come inside," Leo urged. "I don't think Betrys has met Bluebird yet."

Saber strode to the door and opened it to the blue bird Betrys had seen roaming around the resort.

Bluebird strutted inside, gave one anxious honk, and headed for Eva. Leo smiled, as he always did on seeing their pet. Eva and

Saber's pet was an odd-looking bird—sort of a cross between the pictures he'd seen of the extinct dodo bird and a turkey. The bird was a vivid blue with a lighter blue-colored beak and matching legs. Eva and Saber had come across the bird while exploring on the other side of Ione Island, and they'd brought the juvenile bird home with them. During the day, Bluebird wandered the resort, and he spent his evenings with Eva and Saber.

"Meet Bluebird," Eva said, her hand stroking the bird as he cuddled into her.

Betrys grinned. "Ricci would adore him. He's always wanted a pet, but of course, it wasn't possible at the mansion."

"We'll get him a pet," Leo said. "Maybe a puppy. Jerrod's bitch is about to have pups. He'll want to find homes for them."

"What's a puppy?" Betrys asked.

"Bluebird! Leave that jar alone," Eva said.

Bluebird ignored her to stretch his neck and peck at the jar filled with the dead Spiderus. Saber plucked the bird up before placing the container on a higher shelf. He set Bluebird on the floor and the bird strutted over to the shelf, glanced up at the jar, and gave a honk that sounded disappointed.

"A puppy is another Earth creature. I'll take you to visit Jerrod once we're able to move about the resort without worrying about Iseult." Leo grinned at Bluebird's antics.

Leo enjoyed having dinner with his brother and sister-in-law and he thought their presence tamped down some of Betrys's concern for her son.

"Congratulations," Saber said in a low voice when he and Eva were leaving.

"Thanks." Leo glanced at Betrys and saw she was occupied with Bluebird. "I didn't plan it. But it felt right so I went with my gut."

Saber's brows drew together. "She doesn't know."

"Not yet. I thought she had enough to worry about."

"There's a tattoo forming. She'll notice in the morning."

"I know. I'll have to take it slow with her, but it looks as if Ma has her first grandchild," Leo said, and the grin that spread across his lips felt normal instead of forced to hide his true emotions. "He's a great kid, Saber. So serious with eyes that have seen too much. He needs to learn how to play."

"You'll teach him to play," Saber said. "Ma will be beside herself, trying to work out why our mates all bear the mark of the cat."

The laugh that burst from Leo felt good too. "Thanks for coming and bringing dinner."

"I'm just glad you're doing better." Saber drew him in for a quick man-hug.

"Bluebird, are you coming?" Eva asked.

Bluebird honked and remained next to Betrys. Her hand slowed in her petting, and he thumped his head against her leg.

Eva laughed and shook her finger at her pet. "Oh, you faithless creature."

"He can stay," Leo said. "He'll let us know if he wants to leave."

Once they were alone, Betrys turned to Leo. "I like your family. Eva told me she used to own restaurants in the city on Dalcon."

"Casey used to be in the military. There's no reason why you and Ricci can't live here. We're expanding in new directions at every opportunity."

"I'd need to find a job."

"Talk to Saber," Leo said, instinct telling him not to push. Instead, he'd plant the seeds and play a waiting game. No, he'd make love to his mate, take her to bed and seduce her to his way of thinking. Betrys had escaped one prison with Iseult, and he didn't want to make her feel as if he'd placed her in another cage.

Humidity drew beads of sweat to Iseult's forehead as she exited her climate-controlled bungalow. The solar sun had left the sky, and the landscape beyond the resort lay in darkness. Perfect for her men to lie in wait until she requested their aid.

Iseult strode along the gravel path, anger holding her form together and keeping her stomping toward her goal. Somehow, Betrys had seduced one of Pretty's brothers when the brother should have belonged to her. A vein pulsed in sync with her furious footsteps and the crunch of the gravel beneath her *Elsa* designer shoes.

Her nostrils flared as she followed Betrys's scent. Her path took her away from the colored lights and the excited cries and screeches of the women who were attending the dress-up party in the main ballroom. Instead, she pursued her assistant's scent trail, the seductive male aromas that crisscrossed Betrys's direction almost intoxicating with their delicious notes.

The bouquet intensified, almost overpowering her assistant's. Iseult halted and breathed deep to decipher the different layers. She followed a fork to the left and lost the trail.

"Ah," Iseult said with triumph after backtracking. "I have you."

This time, she followed the trail to a building, a separate bungalow. Iseult opened the door and walked inside.

Felix trotted into the ballroom, full of women in fancy dress, and searched for his brother. He found him trying to fend off the advances of a determined alien woman. Her hair tendrils were curled around his older brother's arms, holding him close even as Saber tried to retreat without making a scene. It would've been funny under other circumstances.

"Saber," Felix barked. "Excuse me, ma'am. We have something that needs the boss's attention." Felix signaled for one of their employees, and he hurried over to ask the woman for a dance.

"Thanks. I tried to tell her I was mated, but she wouldn't listen."

"Iseult is on the move," Felix said. "Our guards thought she was coming here, but she's headed toward the private quarters."

"Fuck. Have you alerted Leo?"

"He's not answering. Casey has moved into position." A shrill buzzer started beeping on Felix's wrist unit. "Crap. That's the fence alarm. Wanna bet that it's Iseult's men come to back her up? It's in the south sector."

"On it." Saber spoke into his communicator.

Felix took the opportunity to contact the guards they'd put on Iseult.

"Our security team is on their way," Saber said. "Where is Iseult?"

"Leo's quarters." Felix broke into a run.

CHAPTER FOURTEEN

Leo thrust into Betrys from behind, surrounding her with his strength. Each time they made love, it seemed better. More. She shuddered beneath him, the quakes speeding to her quim and squeezing his cock in rhythmic spasms. Leo nuzzled her neck, his lips moving over the spot on her neck that drove her crazy. He kissed her there, and her heart filled so much she thought she might burst with happiness.

"Leo." His name was a breathy sigh.

"Yes, darling Betrys?"

"Please move. Now." She wriggled forward then slammed back on his cock, and a mew of satisfaction escaped her. He...this...she'd never imagined there would be another man after Corrin. And even if this was for the short term, it showed her there was hope for the future. Her future after Iseult.

"Anything for you, Betrys." He retreated and pushed back

inside her channel, his shaft filling her deeply and massaging every tender spot on the way. His lips fastened on the strange mark that had appeared low down on the side of her neck—the faint black mark that wouldn't seem to scrub away. He sucked hard and the sensations roaring along her veins intensified ten-fold.

"Leo, yes! Yes!" Her quim tightened, flexed and she let out a cry of acute pleasure as she spilled over into climax. Leo surged deep, and she sobbed out his name. He thrust hard again, a primal grunt emerging, his breath misting across her neck. His tongue rasped that spot again, back and forth, back and forth. Another mini orgasm tore through her, and she was vaguely aware of Leo coming.

"Lights on," a hard voice screeched.

"What the fuck?" Leo pulled out of her and whirled around in a defensive crouch. "You can't just walk into someone's home. Get the fuck out."

Iseult. Horror spurted in Betrys, and she rubbed her bare arms. She had to get her robe. Without taking her gaze from Iseult, she slid from the bed, ultra-aware of her nakedness, her vulnerability. This wasn't the way she wanted things to go with Iseult. She'd wanted to make sure Ricci was safe, then disappear without any fuss. Confrontation hadn't been part of her plans. Her hands trembled as she reached for her robe. She *had* to get dressed. Her fingers wrapped around her discarded garment and she forced her locked limbs to work.

"You're dead," Iseult snapped and her furious gaze went from him to fasten on Betrys. She hissed, a sibilant sound spelling danger. "You lied to me."

Iseult's high-pitched screech, her menacing threat, roused Betrys from her fear, and she scrambled into her robe and tied her belt to fasten the clothing securely around her waist. Her acute sense of vulnerability subsided, her pulse rate leveled out, and she edged toward the door.

"What you say?" Iseult demanded, and her skin rippled.

"I did not lie." Betrys slid another step closer to the door, her gaze locked on Iseult while remaining a healthy distance. "You assumed he was dead."

"All others died." Iseult's head cocked, her gaze on Leo. Puzzlement and intrigue shimmered in her voice, but the underlying flatness to her tone bade Betrys to hurry. "Why not he?"

"I didn't lie." Betrys glanced at Leo, interpreted his silent approval, and sidled another step. Iseult couldn't watch them both at once. If she had to split her attention, it might give one of them a chance to raise the alarm.

"You lied by omission," Iseult said and a deep growl issued from low in her chest. Her skin rippled again, and she lost the fight to hold her shape. Her spider form burst outward, and the sharp rent of fabric filled the air. A shrill cry spilled from her throat, and she trembled, her legs shaking before settling on the tiled floor to stabilize her rotund black body. Her chest was a patchwork quilt of vivid green and red and blue, while her face remained in a humanoid form, pale and smooth and beautiful with a skillful application of enhancements, and her black hair in an upswept style.

Ugh. The contrast of beauty and ugliness took creepy to new levels. Betrys couldn't look at her without shuddering, without recalling the acts of murder the woman had committed, without worrying about the murders she might yet commit.

Leo gestured at the door, and Betrys dipped her head in an imperceptible nod.

"What are you doing here, Iseult?" Leo's eyes were long and narrow, and Betrys noticed his hands were clenched, probably to hide his claws. She could see his feline bursting to attack.

But they needed more room. They needed to stall in the hope that help would arrive. She slid nearer to the doorway.

"Stand still." Iseult's voice was a high shriek of rage that made the small hairs at Betrys's nape rise in agitation.

"Why should we?" Leo countered, and he kept moving. "You're the one who's trespassing."

Iseult twisted her head from left to right and back again. "Pretty belongs to me. Not you. You will pay." Another piercing cry rippled from her throat, repeating three times before she fell silent, a gloating smile curving her bright-pink lips. "My men come."

"Lights on," Betrys said in a firm voice from the main room. Sly and Joe were retrieving Ricci. She had to believe that. They would rescue her son.

Bluebird lifted his head from his cushion in the corner and let out an enquiring honk.

"Do you hear me, Bee-trice?" Iseult singsonged. "I have your son. I'm sure he'll taste delicious." She crawled along the floor and shot out into the larger room, stalking Betrys.

"Bitch," Betrys spat, fear at her employer's presence eclipsed by fury. She glared at Iseult. "Ricci has nothing to do with this. He's a child. An innocent." Her gaze speared to Leo. He placed a finger to his lips and reached for his com-circle.

"I see you, Pretty. Leave communicator and come join us out here," Iseult ordered. "Yes, good. Good. You stay while I deal with my traitorous assistant."

"How are you going to deal with me, Iseult?" Betrys's voice cracked toward the end, negating her feisty attitude. She wiped her sweaty palms on her robe and lifted her chin to scowl at her employer. Ex-employer. She was finished working for Iseult. "Kill me in the same way you murdered all those men?"

"Pretty lives." Iseult flicked open her communicator. "Spiderus Mansion."

Hell, the last thing they needed was for Iseult to learn Ricci had disappeared, or even worse, if Iseult ordered security tightened at the mansion.

Without even considering the consequences, Betrys darted forward and knocked the com-circle from Iseult's hand. It clattered onto the tiles and skidded across the floor. Iseult jumped after it and came to a screeching halt, her attention on the jar containing her offspring. She croaked and seemed to shrink, her limbs rounding into her oval Spiderus abdomen.

"Mine? Mine!" she roared.

She whirled to face them, her torso expanding, her legs lifting and stomping on the tiles. *Tap, tap, tap. Tap, tap, tap.* "What you do? Mine. Mine. *Mine.*"

"They were killing Leo." Betrys steeled herself, trying not to let Iseult's anguish get to her. "We cut them out."

Iseult whirled on Betrys. "I will kill your son. I'll suck out his essence and cut him into pieces then put him in a jar and keep him on display."

A guttural roar rushed Betrys's throat, and she whipped the knife Caspar had given her from her pocket. She flew at Iseult, brandishing the knife, with blood pounding in her ears. "You are not hurting my son!" Rage drove her, obscured her vision.

Hack. Slash. *Repeat.*

Hack. Slash. *Repeat.*

She struck repeatedly at one of Iseult's legs and the limb dropped to the floor. Iseult roared and jumped so high her head thumped the ceiling. It must've dazed her because she stumbled on landing.

Hack. Slash. Hack. *Slash. Slash. Slash.*

Iseult leaped at her, knocking her off balance, and her knife went airborne. Betrys hollered, fury rushing up her throat. Something shifted under her skin, and she staggered. Pain—so much pain—slammed her senses. Betrys forced the agony back, groped for her knife.

The blade sliced her palm, and relief soared in her. Her fingers curled around the hilt with a sense of triumph. Chest heaving,

Betrys rolled to her feet, her gaze on Iseult, as she circled ready to attack again.

"Bring it, Spiderus," she growled in a voice that wasn't hers.

"Saber," Leo hollered. "We need you now."

Iseult shrieked and jumped at Betrys. Splotches of purple life force sprayed over the floor. Betrys darted to the side and Leo sprang at Iseult, knocking the Spiderus off balance. The three of them slid on the purple goop and crashed against the wall, sending entertainment vids flying.

"I kill your son and give his corpse to my men." Iseult hissed and waved her leg stump, spraying more purple into the air. "Then put in jar."

Kill. Kill. *Kill.* Betrys hurtled against Iseult, heedless of her own safety. They came together in another angry collision, and the jar containing Iseult's offspring soared through the air. It crashed onto the tiles, exploding on contact. Shards of glass flew, and the vinegar and contents spewed across the floor.

"Holy fuck." Felix gaped at the scene from the doorway.

Bluebird squawked and swooped on the Spiderus egg sac. Two determined pecks later, and Iseult's offspring were gone.

"What the hell?" Saber said. "Did Bluebird just eat that thing?"

"Yeah." Leo pumped his fist in the air. "Go, Bluebird."

"Murder. Murder." Iseult let out an eerie cry. "Kill, kill, *kill.*"

Betrys circled her warily.

Iseult let out a battle cry and ran at Betrys.

"Grab her," Saber said.

"No, stand." Leo stopped his brother. "Betrys needs this."

Betrys ignored the brothers to dart forward and strike out with her knife. Iseult dodged and kicked Betrys's legs out from under her. Pain shot up her spine as her butt hit the ground. She groaned, her vision going weird, and tried to dodge the stomp of one of Iseult's legs.

Betrys jerked to the right and came up in a crouch, her breath see-sawing from her lungs. She faked a right and dove at Iseult, her knife slashing through the air. Iseult went the wrong way. The blade sank into her flesh, forced deeper by Betrys's guiding hand. *Protect Ricci. Kill, kill, kill.*

Iseult faltered. She screamed and kicked out with her legs, trying to dislodge the knife from Betrys's determined grip.

Betrys went airborne, the knife staying put in Iseult's chest. Instinct had her twisting her limbs even before the thought filtered into the right part of her brain. She hit the floor on all fours. Pain, excruciating, like nothing she'd felt before, rippled across her body. She was vaguely aware of Leo and his brothers securing Iseult. Someone crouched beside her, and she flinched until she sucked in a rapid breath and recognized his scent.

Leo.

"Sweetheart," he said, and there was a weird note in his voice. "Breathe. Nice and slow. That's it."

"Hurts." Every muscle shrieked, and her very bones felt as if they were twisting, twisting beyond what was possible and reshaping in a new, unfamiliar way.

"I know it hurts," he murmured, and she drew comfort from his proximity. "Think of a black leopard, sweetheart. Picture me in your mind. Can you do that?"

"Yes," she growled, and her voice sounded weird. She thought of Leo and of stroking his fur. So soft. So pretty. So strong. The pain intensified until she cried out, then black fur sprouted on her arms, her legs. Her robe tore, and agony ripped at her, releasing abruptly. Easing.

"That's it, Betrys. You did good, sweetheart." His hand smoothed over her head, along her back. He tugged away the remnants of her robe.

An uncontrollable tremor seized her, and she swayed, then wrinkled her nose while she stared at her front feet. *Front feet.* Goddess Juna, she had four feet. She had fur. Claws. She ran her tongue over her teeth. Her teeth were lethal weapons. How was this possible? And what if she couldn't change back?

She let out a distressed croak and leaned into Leo.

"Shush, sweetheart. It's all right. You've done the hard part. We'll battle the rest together."

Saber and Felix came to stand beside Leo, their gazes on her, measuring. Maybe bemused? She shuddered and stared at her feet again, her claws. Confusion was the least of her problems now.

"Iseult?" Leo asked, resuming his stroking along her back, his touch comforting and grounding her.

"Dead," Saber said. "Betrys stabbed her in the right place."

Betrys sighed, relief beating out her trembling. Iseult was dead.

"What about her men?"

"The zylon got them. The head of security reported it was the damnedest thing. Their scent seemed to attract the zylons, and the creatures swarmed them. Only two survived before our security team rounded them up." Felix radiated satisfaction. "But not without a fight. One of them lost two legs. No idea if they'll grow back."

Scarlett burst into the room, Casey at her heels. They both skidded to a halt and gaped at the mess in the room.

"Where's Betrys?" Scarlett demanded. "She all right?" Her nostrils flared as she spotted Betrys, still pressed up against Leo. Her brows arched upward. "Betrys?"

"Stand back, Scarlett," Saber ordered. "Don't crowd her. She's terrified enough as it is. Leo, we'll take Betrys to my rooms and talk her through the change back to human."

Felix stepped forward. "Casey and I will clean up here and take care of questioning her men."

"Betrys," Leo murmured.

She rose on hearing his voice and wavered unsteady on her four new legs. Four. No wonder Iseult had wobbled around the web once she'd shifted to her Spiderus form. Extra legs were most disconcerting. She pressed against Leo's legs, her sides heaving as panic threatened to overtake her. What if she couldn't change back?

Leo followed Saber and guided Betrys along the gravel path. His mate could shift. He didn't know how or why, but none of that mattered. The woman both he and his feline had claimed was perfect for them in every way.

She lurched against his legs, and he smoothed his hand over her glossy head, his mouth kicking up into a grin, without him giving the order.

Saber opened the door to a waft of meaty scents. "Company, Eva."

His wife came from the small kitchen, a wooden spoon in her right hand. "Problem?"

Saber's com buzzed, indicating an incoming call. "Hope not. Yeah, Joe? You got the kid?" His brother's shoulders relaxed, and Leo knew it was good news. "Good job. See you soon."

Leo waited until Betrys walked inside and closed the door. He crouched beside her. "Did you hear that, Betrys? Joe and Sly have Ricci. He'll be here soon."

A low rumble sounded in her chest. She stumbled over to a couch, then seemed to realize she was in feline form. Her cry wrung his heart, and he hurried to her.

"Saber and I will help. Don't worry. Everything will work out, sweetheart."

She shook, a low rumble coming from her throat. This had to be confusing for her—hell, it was unheard of in their world. Maybe their mother would have an idea or two, but in most cases, humans or humanoids never shifted, couldn't transform into felines.

"How is this possible, Saber?"

"I've no idea. My best guess is that the genes of our people and Betrys's race work together, are related in some manner. Maybe it was because you bit her. We could do tests—"

"No tests," Leo cut in. "We'll just deal. As long as Betrys and Ricci are safe and Iseult isn't a threat any longer. The rest we can deal with."

Betrys growled, and Leo grinned.

"Betrys," Saber said. "Shifting back to human form is much easier than the initial shift. It's nothing to be frightened of."

"Step by step." Leo kept his gaze on her brown eyes. In her feline form, they bore splotches of amber. Unable to resist, he scratched her behind the ears. "No sweat."

She wrinkled her nose and rose to her feet on shaky legs.

Saber crouched beside her. "Focus your mind, Betrys. Picture your human form. Can you do that?"

Leo stiffened until he realized Saber didn't intend to touch Betrys, and the tension bled from his muscles. Their father had talked them through the change in the same manner. Of course, they'd known what to expect since they'd grown up with knowledge of their heritage. Nothing happened, and Leo frowned. "Picture my brothers walking into this room with your son, Betrys. Think how glad you are that he's safe and how much you want to touch him, to hug him, and reassure yourself that he's here. That he's safe."

Betrys growled, and when Leo placed his hand on her back, her muscles quivered and vibrated beneath his touch.

"That's good," Saber said. "Think of wrapping your arms around your son."

In his peripheral vision, Leo noticed Eva whisk into the bedroom and return with a robe. God, he loved his sisters-in-law. They were both incredible women.

The instant the change took over, going exactly as it should, Leo stepped back to give Betrys room. He and Saber watched, their tension palpable, and Leo's breath eased out when her limbs reshaped into her more familiar form.

The second she knelt naked and whole at his feet, Leo laughed and swooped down to lift her to her feet.

"Here," Eva said. "Put this on."

Leo helped her don the robe and noted the defined black cat tattoo at her mating site. Satisfaction filled him, made his smile widen, made him want to scoop her into his arms and lay a possessive kiss on her rosy lips. He did none of that, giving her space instead.

A honk came from outside the door.

"Better let Bluebird inside," Leo said. "He's a hero."

"He distracted Iseult." Betrys stared at her fingers as if ascertaining they were back to normal. "Is she really dead?"

"She'll never hurt anyone again," Saber said and opened the door to let the chubby blue bird walk inside. "I thought Iseult was gonna lose it when Bluebird gobbled down her offspring. I hope Bluebird doesn't suffer any ill effects."

"Ugh! Bluebird ate those things?" Eva pulled a face. "How? Last I saw, they were in a jar."

Saber explained, then said, "I'm not sure what we'll do with her men. Two survived the zylon attacks."

Betrys wrinkled her nose, risked a glance at Leo then focused on her hands again. "Zylons?"

"Cute fluffy creatures with a poisonous bite," Leo said, his scrutiny intense. She hadn't mentioned her unexpected shift yet "It's the reason we have the fence around the resort, to keep our guests safe."

"What do you think we should do with the two guards, Betrys?" Saber asked the question, and they all stared at her, waiting for her reply.

"Ricci is safe now?" Betrys studied their faces in a search for reassurance. "Your brothers are bringing him here to the resort?"

"He's on his way," Saber confirmed.

"I need to find a new home," Betrys said. "A job."

"You—" Leo broke off as Eva's fingers squeezed his forearm, her nails digging into his flesh like sharp talons.

"I hoped you'd stay and take a job here," Eva said. "I need administrative help with menu planning and purchases, and I know that Scarlett is stretched thin in reception. She needs more time to do the special tasks that Saber sets her. The poor girl hasn't had a day off for ages. There are other children here, and we have the beginnings of a school. It would be good for your son to play with others his own age. What do you say? Will you stay?"

Leo held his breath and waited for Betrys to speak. He refused to let her leave. She just didn't understand that yet. Saber and Eva knew, but they thought Betrys deserved a choice. There was no choice for him. If she insisted on leaving, he would go with her.

A crease formed on Betrys's forehead, and she focused on him. "Why did I turn into a cat? Will it happen again?"

"I—we—don't know for sure, but I suspect it is because I bit you. I didn't know this would happen, but I'm not sorry." Even he heard the note of defiance, backed by determination, in his voice. "I've come to like and admire you, Betrys."

"Even after what I did?" she whispered.

"Yes. I want you and Ricci to stay." Fuck, he loved her. Now that Iseult was gone, he needed to woo her around to his way of thinking. The addition of a child thrilled him, filling him with a wave of joy. "Ma would enjoy having another child around the resort."

Betrys nodded—finally—and his breath eased out in an audible hiss. "We can stay for a while, see how things work out. Maybe reading my cards will help."

A knock came at the door, and Felix and Casey entered.

"Your room is clear," Felix said. "We've taken away the broken furniture."

"Iseult?" Saber asked.

"It was the weirdest thing." Felix shook his head. "All the

Spiderus bodies faded away until there was nothing but piles of black dust."

"Several races do this on death," Betrys commented. "They believe they go back to nature and await another rebirth."

"God forbid," Leo muttered. "The idea of Iseult returning is gonna give me nightmares. Felix, Casey, thanks for the cleanup. I'm knackered." He caught Betrys in a yawn. "You look tired too, sweetheart. Come on." He wrapped his arm around her waist and urged her toward the door, but she balked.

"I want to see Ricci."

"I'll contact Joe and Sly and ask them to escort Ricci to Leo's rooms as soon as they land," Saber said.

"Promise?" Her tone was fierce, and something squeezed in Leo's chest. His little warrior.

"You have my word. They won't arrive until morning," Saber added. "You can meet them yourself."

Betrys gave a curt nod and let Leo guide her outside.

"Your siblings are fun," she said. "I wish I had a family like yours."

She did, Leo thought. She just didn't understand it yet.

CHAPTER FIFTEEN

They were free.

No longer would Iseult's threats hover over their lives. The heady sense of freedom filled Betrys from the moment she opened her eyes. She edged out of the sleep-bed, away from Leo's warmth, and looked for her robe. When she couldn't find it, she grabbed one of Leo's shirts and tugged it over her head. It smelled of him—of musk and sunshine and some sort of cleanser with a perfume she couldn't identify—and the scent soothed her, made her feel happy.

"Why are you awake?" Leo's husky voice sent an enjoyable frisson soaring to her sex.

"Couldn't sleep any longer. I thought I'd be sore today with lots of cuts and bruises. There are none—well, nothing that's too bad." Betrys watched Leo. She hadn't dreamed about turning into a black cat. A blip in her feel-good mood since she couldn't decide if this was a good or a bad thing. On the negative side, the change hurt. A lot. She stretched, lifting onto the balls of her feet, tested her physique. A new strength rippled in her muscles, her body. Not a bad thing, since she had Ricci to protect.

"Looking good in my T-shirt, sweetheart." Leo climbed out of the sleep-bed and strode toward her. His arms went around her, and he tugged her against his chest.

Home, she thought, his scent filling her senses.

"You've seen me in my feline form, Betrys."

She tugged and freed herself so she could watch his face. "Yes."

"I like you. A lot," he said, and a strange expression slid across his face.

Something in her, some sixth sense that hadn't been present before, told her he wasn't telling her the truth. There was more, so she waited.

"When I bit you here, on the neck." His fingers traced across the spot that bore the tiny cat tattoo. "I marked you, claimed you."

"Claimed me?" Warmth spread across her skin, and Betrys realized she liked—loved—the idea. She didn't feel coerced or threatened. It was more a sense of him accepting everything she was—both good and bad. And there had been a lot of bad.

"I want you, Betrys. I want to raise Ricci as my son. I want to live with you, love you, and maybe have more children. I want to build a life with you."

"Even after everything I've done?"

"You were trying to survive and keep your son safe. Betrys, I would have done the same thing. So would my brothers. I admit that at first I wanted revenge, but once I met Ricci and understood you were just doing your best to keep him safe, everything changed for me. We can take things as slow as you want, but I warn you now. I'm determined. I'm stubborn, and I will get my way. We will be together. A family."

He sounded sure of himself. Confident, and she liked that about him. Yet she'd seen the way he and his brothers valued women too. They listened to them, sought their opinions and let them take an active part in the running of the resort. While she'd loved Corrin, he'd never, ever asked her advice.

"We can start by making love," he said when she didn't say anything, couldn't say anything because emotion backed up her throat.

"But Ricci will be here soon."

"My brothers will let us know." Leo flashed a grin that made her heart stutter. "Besides, with a kid around, we should get used to bedroom interruptions."

Betrys laughed and Leo swung her into his arms and carried her back to the sleep-bed.

"Will I change into a cat again?" Goddess, it had hurt so much. It had felt as if her body was turning itself inside out.

"If you will it," Leo said. "Think of the fun we could have together, playing in the surf, running along the beach at night."

"It hurt."

"The change never feels comfortable, but it does become easier and faster with practice. Your first transformation was driven by fear and rage, and you didn't have the training, the knowledge that my brothers and sister and I were brought up with. Now that we know you're capable of shifting, we can help and offer advice, but don't worry. You can shift when you're ready." Leo paused. "You will always be a feline now, Betrys. The ability to shift and the things that come with being a feline will never go away."

Once again, she compared Leo to Corrin. If Corrin had known she could do this, he would have insisted on her changing so he could record the phenomenon. He wouldn't have considered her feelings, her objections, her doubts. She thought about the fun she'd had playing with Leo at the beach. "I'll consider your words."

"Good. Let's seal our bargain with a kiss."

"What bargain?"

"Your promise to think about trying another shift. Your promise to stay at Middlemarch Resort with me."

He didn't give her a chance to ask another question, to refute his words or even turn them over in her mind. His mouth settled over hers and she sighed at the wash of pure pleasure that swept her at his touch. Since her shift, her senses seemed to work overtime—another thing to ask Leo.

For now, she followed her gut instinct and kissed Leo in return, running her hands over his hard muscles.

"T-shirt off," he muttered.

The removal took longer than it should have, since Leo explored a faint bruise on her stomach, kissed it tenderly, then his calloused hands shaped her breasts. He ran his tongue around her nipples, teasing them to hard points before he whipped the T-shirt over her head.

"Everything smells more," Betrys said. "I feel as if my senses are exploding. I can hear better too." Her gaze connected with his. "I will always be like this now."

"Is that a bad thing? If you stay here, you'll be amongst others of your kind. We—I—can help you since this stuff is second nature to me."

"I'll think about everything you've said and discuss the matter with Ricci. My son should have a say."

"Good, enough talking now," Leo said, and he made sure by sealing his mouth over hers and kissing her until she was breathless.

She ran her hands down his back and let them settle on his muscled backside. "Turn over," she demanded, urgency thrumming her now. "I want to be on top of you."

"Well. I'm enjoying this new bossy side."

Betrys laughed and pushed at his shoulder. Then she was straddling his hips, exploring his flat nipples with her fingers and mouth. Laughter tickled her as she teased him by rubbing against his cock while pretending her interest lay elsewhere.

This, the passion that simmered between them, was so much more than she'd imagined, more than she'd deserved or ever hoped to secure.

"I want to be inside you, Betrys. You can take me. I can smell your arousal."

She sucked in a deep breath, part of her still surprised by the layers of scents she could identify now. Among them were his musky scent and the slightly sweeter one belonging to her. She lifted her hips and took him inside her, going much slower than her mind wanted to prolong the pleasure of his cock stretching her sheath. When he filled her, she paused and studied his features. His teeth were gritted, his expression one of pain.

"Oh, am I hurting you?"

"If you don't start moving, I might get inspired to spank you." His hand slid up her upper thigh to pinch her butt.

The nip of his fingers made her chuckle, but she did start moving, riding him in an easy pace and experimenting with the angles that produced the best friction.

"Such a pretty sight."

"Looks good from this end too. Oh, oh!" Betrys began to move faster, straining to follow the shards of pleasure bursting through her quim. Two more quick rise-and-fall movements and she came in a fast climax. Almost before the spasms tailed off, Leo had rolled them and loomed over her, his green eyes full of humor.

He thrust into her, stealing a kiss before laying a trail of kisses down her neck and heading inexorably toward the tiny cat tattoo. Her heart gave three extra hard beats while her breath hitched in expectation of the pleasure she knew would soar through her at his touch.

Her arms went around him, and she nuzzled his neck. A strange sensation froze her for an instant until she realized it was the start of a shift. Something weird was going on with her eyes, while her teeth were much sharper. When Leo continued to kiss her and strum his tongue over the tattoo, she relaxed. With his good senses, he'd know what was happening to her. Nothing to worry about. Obviously.

She kissed the spot where his neck met his shoulder, then licked the same spot. Leo groaned, and she felt the pulse of his cock deep in her quim.

Betrys nipped him, and Leo cried out, shuddering and trembling as if he couldn't control his limbs. Instinct guided her, and before she knew it, she was biting him, the taste of his coppery blood filling her mouth.

Leo's hips moved, the base of his cock hitting her clit as he withdrew and invaded her body again. She licked away the blood, the taste of him strangely comforting, strangely sweet.

Leo thrust into her once more, and she exploded into pleasure. She was aware of a scream, a masculine shout as the ecstasy took her under into a place ruled by sensations.

When her mind settled, the first thing she saw was the happiness wreathing Leo's face, his broad smile and glittering eyes.

"What?"

"You claimed me."

She stared at him before understanding forged into her orgasm-buzzed brain. "I bit you."

"Your feline claimed me as your mate."

Betrys scowled. "Yeah. So? Is that bad?"

"I think it's very, very good, and I'm so happy I could burst. I love you, Betrys."

His heartfelt words shifted something inside her, and his declaration brought joy. "Leo."

Seconds later, they were kissing, mouths seeking mouths, mating sites and every bit of available flesh.

Only Leo's com-circle drove them up for air. He picked up. "Yeah?"

"Sly and Joe are almost here. They'll land in ten minutes,"

Saber informed him, and Betrys heard his words without difficulty. "Thought you'd want to know."

"Thanks." Leo rolled out of the sleep-bed.

Betrys was out and halfway to the cleansing room. She stopped, her gaze going to the spot where she'd bitten him. Instead of an angry wound, a tiny black cat had formed. "You have a tattoo, the same as mine."

"I can't wait to show Ma," Leo said. "She'll be so happy."

As she hurriedly cleaned and dressed, she thought of Leo's words, of his request for her to stay. She wanted to, she realized. She wanted it very much, but first, she needed to consult with Ricci. He'd seemed to like Leo on the dreamscape, but she wanted to ensure he enjoyed the resort before she committed. Although she hadn't thought of an alternative, she was certain she would find one or two if she searched.

The shuttle had landed by the time they arrived. Saber and Eva, Felix and Casey, Scarlett and their mother Anna were all there to meet them, despite the fact the solar sun hadn't risen yet.

One of Leo's brothers walked off the shuttle and Ricci followed.

"Ricci!" Betrys shouted and she found herself running faster and more freely than she ever had before. She scooped her son into her arms and hugged him hard.

"Mother, you're hurting me."

"Sorry." She released him and studied his face. "Are you all right?"

Ricci smiled. He actually smiled and her heart squeezed with love and relief. "Joe and Sly told me all about the resort. There are children who are the same age as me and I can swim in the sea. Will we live here now?"

Leo came to stand beside her and slipped his arm around her waist. "Would you like that?"

"Yes," Ricci said.

"I think we should have breakfast." Anna Mitchell stepped

forward. "Pancakes, I think. This seems like a pancake kind of day."

"What's a pancake?" Ricci asked.

Betrys smiled. "I don't know."

"It's an Earth food," Leo said. "You'll find them delicious. I promise."

"Betrys?"

She turned to see Sly and another man. This must be Joe—the only Mitchell sibling she hadn't yet met. His green eyes, shaggy black hair, and muscular build told of the blood relationship. They were twins, although their different hairstyles made it easy to tell them apart.

"Thank you." She gave them both a swift hug and ignored Leo's low growl of protest. "Thank you for bringing Ricci to me."

"We got your currency for you," Sly replied.

"And something else we thought you might like from Ricci's room," Joe spoke this time.

"That's Ricci's drawing book," Betrys said.

Leo's brother smiled. "Look at the pictures inside."

She sought Ricci and found him walking with Leo's mother and chattering away, so she accepted the book and opened it. A gasp escaped as she stared at the pictures her son had drawn.

"What is it?" Leo asked.

Betrys showed him Ricci's picture of two black cats, one larger than the other. They were running on a beach, the jade-green water beyond, and Ricci had drawn himself in the picture, racing alongside the two cats with a big smile on his face.

Leo turned the pages and there were other pictures, drawn in different places around the resort, but all showing the same thing. Two black cats and a small boy. Ricci.

Tears blurred her vision and a tightness sealed her throat, making her swallow several times before she could speak.

"Well," she said. "It looks as if we're staying."

Leo swooped her off her feet and swung her around and around, his joyous laughter loud enough to halt his family and draw their attention. "Betrys and Ricci are staying." He set her on her feet and kissed her—a hard, possessive kiss that she felt all the way to her toes.

"Of course we're staying," Ricci said.

Betrys and Leo turned toward her son and recommenced walking, their arms wrapped around each other.

"We're a family," Ricci said to Betrys.

"We are," Leo agreed, his love shining in his face for her and his family to see. "Let's have pancakes."

Would you like to read more of my romances? Sign up for my newsletter (https://shelleymunro.com/newsletter/) to learn about upcoming releases, receive free books and short stories tied to my series plus contest and special promotion news.

Also, I want to ask a favor. Word-of-mouth is crucial for an author to succeed. If you enjoyed this book, please consider leaving a review. Even if it's only a few lines, it would be a big help.

Middlemarch Shifters is the original series and features the ancestors of the characters in the Middlemarch Capture romances. Please turn the page to glimpse *My Assassin*, where you'll meet Leo's forebear of the same name.

EXCERPT – MY ASSASSIN

BOOK 4, MIDDLEMARCH SHIFTERS

L eo wandered through the doors of the Queenstown casino, every sense alert for his mate. Even though he had no idea of her identity, he suspected it was the mystery blonde woman who had helped Sylvie—Felix and Tomasine's daughter—during her first unexpected change to feline. Sylvie had taken everyone unaware when she'd shifted for the first time at age five instead of the normal age of sixteen. It was lucky the unidentified blonde had been around to help the confused youngster.

After sifting through the jingle of the slots and loud chatter, plus the layered scents of perfume, cologne, and pure excitement at the casino, Leo headed for the bar.

He'd arrived the previous evening and prowled the surrounds of Queenstown without luck, chafing at the denser population. He hadn't caught the faintest whiff of his mystery woman, and that made him yearn to shift to black leopard and run free across the hills to relieve his frustration.

It wasn't as if he could grab the nearest willing female and fuck the disappointment away, not when the female he desired was his mate. Damn woman. She'd mucked up his sex life but good. Leo snarled under his breath, cursing the fates and the heat prickling across his skin.

Without warning, Leo caught an elusive scent. A familiar one, it bore a hint of spiciness, reminding him of the wildflowers and grasses that bloomed around the salt lake in spring. He halted and almost caused a pileup of eager punters behind.

"Sorry," he said, stepping aside to allow the impatient patrons to pass and head for their gambling game of choice. He sniffed the air again. A mixture of strong perfumes and colognes. A whiff of body odor and musk and a hint of wildflowers.

It was his mate.

She was here.

Leo's heart squeezed out an exuberant pump, and he strode between the roulette tables, following the trail, his mood improving with his discovery. With no clear idea of her appearance, he scanned faces of women—both young and old. Up ahead, he saw a slim form dressed in a black halter dress. The line of her naked back drew his attention, as did the gentle sway of her hips. Her fragrance.

His.

Leo quickened his pace until he stood right behind her. She had brown hair with reddish strands, not the blonde he'd seen or others had mentioned. A frown creased his brow. Maybe she wore wigs. Tonight her hair piled on top of her head in a complicated twist, the type that made a man hesitate and wonder if it were safe to touch. In the past, he'd made the wrong decision and suffered the consequences.

The woman ignored his presence, continuing her elegant and

sexy sway while she progressed through the crowded room.

Damn. This mating business was tricky. More convoluted than he'd envisioned. *Show his face. Attraction. One becomes two—a couple.* Huh! Witnessing Saber's courtship of Emily and Felix's adventures with Tomasine should've alerted him to potential pitfalls. Like a fool, he'd relied on his natural charm and looks to ease him through without mishap. *Not working.*

The woman sashayed toward the bar, his original destination, so Leo followed while deciding how to approach her. Did he use a corny pick-up line, or did he bowl up to her and say, "You're my mate. Let's fuck and get acquainted?"

He snorted. Yeah, brashness would snag her interest all right—if she didn't run screaming for the cops first.

A man appeared in front of his woman. He spoke to her. Leo gaped in consternation when the tall male kissed her. And it wasn't a peck either. Tongue came into play.

Hell.

What did he do now?

His hands curled to fists, and he had to restrain his urge to choke the living daylights out of the male groping his woman.

She pulled away and laughed. Low and husky, the chortle twisted his gut and brought a wave of envy. Could a female mate with two different men? Leo sifted through the mating facts as relayed by Saber. There weren't that many, and nothing he'd learned had prepared him for this dilemma. His younger twin brothers were both chasing Maggie, but they were a law unto themselves. They didn't report in often, so their experiences were no help.

Leo forced himself to walk past to the bar. He slid onto a vacant barstool and ordered a dark beer. Meanwhile, the couple entered the adjoining restaurant. A hostess directed them to a table in Leo's range of sight—if he craned his neck. They settled and accepted a wine list from the waitress. After handing over a twenty-dollar note and receiving his change, Leo shifted his barstool along the bar for a better view, sipped his drink and watched them with a mixture of irritation and pique.

The woman glanced up as if sensing his observation. Leo didn't look away but held her gaze, letting instinct guide him. Instead of glaring at him or glancing away, she returned his interest. A small smile played around her full lips. Her friend tapped her on the shoulder, but she didn't return her attention to him straightaway. She winked at Leo before turning away to accept the menu.

Leo let out a breath, even more confused. He didn't know what to think or how to act. His logical mind, anyhow. His unruly body had this bit memorized, and he shifted on the barstool to ease into a more comfortable position.

Leo continued to watch the couple. After consulting the wine list, they turned their attention to the menu. The woman scanned the dishes on offer and set her menu on the table. The male read it through, asked his companion questions, and appeared to dither.

Score one point against him, Leo thought with disgruntlement. The stranger was good-looking with sandy-colored hair, or at least Leo had glimpsed other female diners checking him out and exchanging whispers. He was taller than the mystery woman and possessed hulking shoulders, although the suit jacket might hide a paunch.

Leo grunted. Mate or not?

Uncertainty made him reach for his drink. *Damn. Empty.* He signaled to the bartender and received another beer. After a third drink, Leo decided he was both sad and mistaken. This woman couldn't be his mate. He drained the last mouthful from his glass and stood. With a final glance, he turned and walked away.

Outside the casino, night had fallen despite the long summer evenings. A soft breeze ruffled his hair, bringing with it a whiff of exotic spices and Chinese food. Leo strode toward the lake, deciding if he couldn't shift and run, at least he could walk. When he passed restaurants lining the road, he heard flirtation, laughter, saw couples everywhere, their seats shoved close, heads together. Soft whispers.

Acute loneliness assailed him, joining the edgy anger and irritation bubbling inside. Poetic justice, according to his brothers, because women had fallen at his feet since he'd gone through the change as a teenager. His pretty face, everyone said.

Just as well he was here on his own, not with his brothers. Leo gave a wry grin before sobering. He could imagine the ribbing they'd give him. Nope. This was one of the times when solitary was good even if he reeled in confusion.

As he neared the edge of Lake Wakatipu, a tourist boat pulled up at the jetty. Passengers drifted off the boat in pairs. Leo's throat tightened, and he shifted his attention to the dark surface of the lake instead. Around the shore, lights twinkled while darkness shrouded the Remarkable mountain range that bordered the large expanse of water. Leo kept walking until the sounds of high spirits faded. Now and then, a vehicle passed, or he caught the drift of chatter and music from an open window. More couples. *Queenstown—a regular Noah's ark.*

Despondent, he continued to walk until he left the main center behind. Usually, the countryside soothed, relaxed him, but not tonight. He'd come out here to think, but nothing could get past the fact that the woman he wanted was with another man. Without being bigheaded, he knew he could woo and win another one, except his heart...his heart might break accepting second best.

Still out of sorts, Leo threw stones into the lake, the dull plop when the stone sank beneath the water echoing in his mind. He sat on the cool ground and studied the horizon with its myriad twinkling lights. After setting off from Middlemarch with such hopes, he'd plummeted to rock bottom.

"Hell, any minute I'm gonna break out with the country music." In disgust, Leo leapt to his feet to walk back to central

Queenstown and his hotel. He'd paid for the room, so might as well use it. Instead of staying for the entire weekend, he'd check out tomorrow morning and return to Middlemarch. He needed advice, and he figured he'd find someone at home. Emily, since she specialized in sympathy instead of teasing.

Twenty minutes later, Leo walked into the foyer of his boutique hotel. It was exclusive and overlooked the water. He liked staying in the Wallace because the staff was friendly and efficient, the owner a fellow shifter, a widow whose husband had died in a car accident. Erin was older than him. Gorgeous and sexy, he wished she'd been the one instead of the mystery woman. They'd considered a fling, but with no spark between them, they'd left it at close friends.

"Hi, Leo," the night receptionist chirped.

He lifted a hand in greeting but kept walking. Instead of using the lifts, he climbed the stairs to his third-floor room. He plucked his keycard from his pocket and entered.

The faint scent of lemon polish and shifter combined with a foreign one—a hint of delicate flowers and a touch of spicy greenery. The maid had turned down his bed and placed a chocolate mint on his pillow. She'd forgotten to leave on the bedside lamp, which was a no-no in Erin's rules. The hotel proprietress liked to get the small details right.

Leo shut the door, pausing a moment to let his eyes adjust to the pitch-black. The faint rustle coming from the bed made him pause. He peered through the darkness, picked out the shape of a person and cursed under his breath. He didn't have the wrong room. The maid was going beyond the call of duty.

"Whoever you are, get out of my room. If you leave now, I won't report you to Erin." Leo sounded testy, but it had been that sort of day. He didn't have the energy to dredge up smooth, urbane, and charming.

"I'll go if you want," a husky voice said. "But don't you want to see what you're rejecting first?"

The woman had the music of Europe in her speech. French or Italian. Something continental and familiar.

"Turn on the light." Leo held his breath, distrusting his senses.

The crisp cotton sheets rustled. Leo's heart raced. This was his mate, and she was waiting in his bed. His lungs expanded while he tried to exert control on his body. Not a single thought of cold showers or icky situations worked on his eager dick. It felt as if every drop of blood had sunk to his groin while he waited for illumination.

After a soft, descriptive curse that raised a grin in Leo, she found the light. It flicked on, spotlighting the bed. Leo gaped. The female in his bed wasn't wearing anything except a come-hither smile.

It was her—the mystery woman.

Who is this woman? Learn more now
https://shelleymunro.com/books/my-assassin/

ALSO BY SHELLEY

Middlemarch Shifters
My Scarlet Woman
My Younger Lover
My Peeping Tom
My Assassin
My Estranged Lover
My Feline Protector
My Determined Suitor
My Cat Burglar
My Stray Cat
My Second Chance
My Plan B
My Cat Nap
My Romantic Tangle
My Blue Lady
My Twin Trouble
My Precious Gift
My Grumpy Wolf

Middlemarch Gathering
My Highland Mate
My Highland Fling
My Elusive Mate
My Valiant Princess
My Highland Wedding
My Highland Billionaire

Middlemarch Capture
Snared by Saber
Favored by Felix
Lost with Leo
Spellbound with Sly
Journey with Joe
Star-Crossed with Scarlett

House of the Cat
Captured & Seduced
Claimed & Seduced
Merry & Seduced
Stranded & Seduced
Seized & Seduced
Hunted & Seduced
Festive & Seduced
Betrayed & Seduced
Enticed & Seduced

Dragon Investigators
Blue Moon Dragon
Blood Moon Dragon
Black Moon Dragon
Snow Moon Dragon

About Author

USA Today bestselling author Shelley Munro lives in Auckland, the City of Sails, with her husband and a cheeky Jack Russell/mystery breed dog.

Typical New Zealanders, Shelley and her husband left home for their big OE soon after they married (translation of New Zealand speak - big overseas experience). A twelve-month-long adventure lengthened to six years of roaming the world. Enduring memories include being almost sat on by a mountain gorilla in Rwanda, lazing on white sandy beaches in India, whale watching in Alaska, searching for leprechauns in Ireland, and dealing with ghosts in an English pub.

While travel is still a big attraction, these days Shelley is most likely found in front of her computer following another love - that of writing stories of contemporary and paranormal romance and adventure. Other interests include watching rugby (strictly for research purposes), cycling, playing croquet and the ukelele, and curling up with an enjoyable book.

Visit Shelley at her website.
https://shelleymunro.com/

Sign Up for Shelley's Newsletter
https://shelleymunro.com/newsletter/